'Believe what yo

'I don't have to just
account of myself t
'There's been nothing unprofessional between myself and Dr Kapinsky.' That at least was true—during working hours.

'He's very discreet, so I've heard,' Jarrad drawled, keeping his voice low so that no one else could possibly hear. 'I can't believe that he would have passed you up. Even I have to admit that you're quite something. Just don't use it to gain any leverage while we're up north—with me or anyone else. It won't wash. When it's just you and me up north, when we're out of this place, we won't be playing any games, believe me! Don't you forget it!'

Rebecca Lang trained to be a State Registered Nurse in Kent, England, where she was born. Her main focus of interest became operating theatrework, and she gained extensive experience in all types of surgery on both sides of the Atlantic. Now living in Toronto, Canada, she is married to a Canadian pathologist, and has three children. When not writing, Rebecca enjoys gardening, reading, theatre, exploring new places, and anything to do with the study of people.

Recent titles by the same author:
WEDDING SONG
MIDNIGHT SUN

THE SURGEON'S DECISION

BY
REBECCA LANG

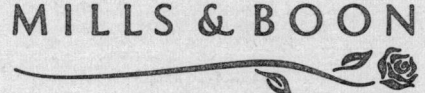

MILLS & BOON

DID YOU PURCHASE THIS BOOK WITHOUT A COVER?
If you did, you should be aware it is **stolen property** as it was reported *unsold and destroyed* by a retailer. Neither the Author nor the publisher has received any payment for this book.

All the characters in this book have no existence outside the imagination of the author, and have no relation whatsoever to anyone bearing the same name or names. They are not even distantly inspired by any individual known or unknown to the author, and all the incidents are pure invention.

All rights reserved including the right of reproduction in whole or in part in any form. This edition is published by arrangement with Harlequin Enterprises II B.V. The text of this publication or any part thereof may not be reproduced or transmitted in any form or by any means, electronic or mechanical, including photocopying, recording, storage in an information retrieval system, or otherwise, without the written permission of the publisher.

This book is sold subject to the condition that it shall not, by way of trade or otherwise, be lent, resold, hired out or otherwise circulated without the prior consent of the publisher in any form of binding or cover other than that in which it is published and without a similar condition including this condition being imposed on the subsequent purchaser.

*MILLS & BOON, the Rose Device and
LOVE ON CALL are trademarks of the publisher.
Harlequin Mills & Boon Limited,
Eton House, 18-24 Paradise Road, Richmond, Surrey TW9 1SR*

© Rebecca Lang 1996

ISBN 0 263 79544 6

*Set in Times 10 on 11 pt. by
Rowland Phototypesetting Limited
Bury St Edmunds, Suffolk*

03-9605-50996

Made and printed in Great Britain

CHAPTER ONE

'CODE one hundred. Code one hundred. Room 529, Edith Cavell Wing. Repeat, 529, Edith Cavell. Paging Dr Jarrad Lucas, Dr Claud Moreau, Dr Laurel Harte.' The disembodied voice issuing from the intercom system sounded eerily loud in the wide hospital corridor that was empty on the quiet Sunday afternoon.

'Oh...damn!' Dr Laurel Harte halted abruptly in the corridor and spun round on a heel to face the other way. 'I should have known it was too good to be true.'

She muttered to herself with a weary resignation as she began to retrace her steps, speeding up as she went, heading towards the nearest bank of elevators that would take her down to basement level where she could take the underground passage to the Edith Cavell Wing. That was the quickest way to get there. Code one hundred was the cardiac arrest code.

The bags that she was carrying hampered her progress; one was her medical bag, filled with everything she would need for a cardiac arrest and any other medical emergency, the other a large attaché case that was stuffed with the last of her papers and books from her shared office in the hospital.

She had had to clear out; this was her last working day at University Hospital in Gresham, Ontario. She had agreed to take the afternoon call on the cardiac arrest team for a friend and colleague who had been called to the operating-rooms in a hurry as part of a kidney transplant team. For a while she had thought she could get away with little to do of a professional nature.

'Come on! Come on!' Laurel Harte jabbed impatiently at the call button when she reached the elevators breathlessly. She pushed back her untidy, fine dark hair that clung about her pale, delicate face in feminine wisps, before looking desperately at her wristwatch. At the sound of Dr Jarrad Lucas's name, too, her stomach muscles had clenched painfully. She was not looking forward to another run-in with him over how things should be done.

'Room 529. . .' She whispered the numbers to herself. That was on the fifth floor, Mr Foley's room—Joshua Kapinsky's patient, waiting for heart surgery next week. . .

Once inside an elevator, moving down, Laurel thought about Mr Foley, the man in his fifties who was in hospital to have a coronary artery bypass operation later that week. At least, he *was* to have had it. For some time now he had been having chest pains, angina because of a partial block in his coronary artery.

The operation planned for him would essentially have given him an additional artery to supply the heart muscle with blood, would have relieved the pain. But it looked now as though the disease had pre-empted the surgical team and he had suffered a cardiac arrest.

Laurel had come to know Mr Foley well during the few days of his pre-operative work-up, and during the times that she had met him in the out patient department and in Dr Kapinsky's private office in the hospital.

As she hurried along the fifth floor corridor of the Edith Cavell wing towards room 529 she saw Dr Claud Moreau, the senior medical resident, with his intern and the anaesthesia intern, coming towards her from the other end. The anaesthesia staff man would be on his way, as would the two respiratory technologists who were on the team. Then she heard an elevator door open and close behind her. That would be Jarrad Lucas. She did not look round.

Room 529, when she entered it, was a scene of ordered activity, with an atmosphere of tension held in check. Two nurses were present—one giving external cardiac massage, one bending over Mr Foley's head ready to push air into his lungs manually via a plastic airway tube that was already in his mouth and attached to a large balloon-shaped bag.

Laurel caught a glimpse of Mr Foley's grey face as she quickly squeezed by the bed to get to the top of it, where the metal bedhead had been removed and propped against the wall. She wanted to get the endotracheal tube in place before Jarrad Lucas was there, breathing down her neck. The familiar churning inside her began again as her thoughts focused momentarily on her colleague, who would at this moment be striding along the corridor towards her.

While the nurse steadied Mr Foley's head Laurel inserted a laryngoscope into his mouth, flexing his jaw so that she could see down his throat with the light. Silently the nurse handed her an endotracheal tube, and in seconds she had it in place. The patient could be permanently brain-damaged within a few minutes without oxygen.

As she straightened up Dr Claud Moreau and the two interns entered the room, closely followed by Dr Jarrad Lucas. Very briefly Laurel's eyes met the assessing glance of Dr Lucas as he took in what she was doing. They both watched while the nurse switched on the portable ventilator, and in a moment their patient was being ventilated. There was still no discernible heartbeat.

Laurel felt herself stiffen with an anticipatory tension that had little to do with the job in hand.

'Everything all right this end?' Dr Lucas's calm

question caused her to look up again to where he was standing beside her. There was something about his cool, perceptive grey eyes under dark brows, about his lean, intelligent, attractive face that always left her feeling slightly nonplussed, even though she had worked with him for some time. That time had been fraught with emotional sparks and tension.

'Yes,' she answered tightly, checking the oxygen gauge.

While the medical intern took over the external cardiac massage from the tired nurse Dr Lucas prepared to inject a stimulant drug directly into the heart muscle, and Dr Moreau got ready to place the electric defibrillator paddles on Mr Foley's chest, to shock his heart into renewed life.

'Xylocaine drip ready?' someone asked. The anaesthesia staff man arrived then, together with the rest of the team.

'Don't go away, Laurel, I want to talk to you.' The quiet command from Dr Lucas, carefully without inflexion, caused Laurel to pause in the doorway of room 529 as she was leaving. 'Wait for me.'

When Dr Lucas joined her in the corridor they walked together towards the elevators, their white lab coats flapping over identical green scrub suits. Wordlessly he took the heavier of her two bags from her, while she relinquished it with a slight shrug.

There seemed to be a certain irony in his gallant gesture, and she clenched her jaw in an effort to bite back the sarcastic retort that had been on the tip of her tongue. After all, she still had to work with the guy again in the near future—albeit in a vastly different setting.

'Well. . . Mr Foley won't be having his operation as scheduled,' Jarrad Lucas murmured, echoing Laurel's own thoughts as he strode along the corridor beside her. Not short herself, his towering height made her feel like a midget.

'No...' Laurel agreed soberly, trying hard to be civilised, professional. 'At least he's alive.'

They had succeeded in resuscitating Mr Foley, had remained on the scene until it was quite clear that he was all right before dispersing the emergency team. Others would take over from then on, others from the highly specialised cardiac team of which she was no longer a member. She felt exhausted now that the adrenalin high was beginning to recede.

'Maybe they'll get on with the coronary bypass this evening—do an angiogram first, provided he's stabilised,' Dr Lucas commented. 'What do you think?'

'Surely you're not interested in my opinion,' she said, unable to contain herself.

He smiled then, as though at some secret joke at her expense. 'Where we're going we'll need to... confer, shall I say?'

'I intend to keep you to that,' she replied grimly.

Two other staff members joined them as they waited for the elevator. 'Any regrets about leaving?' Dr Lucas queried politely, no doubt for the benefit of the others who were within earshot. 'It must seem odd not to be part of that team any more.'

'Oh...there are always some regrets,' she said carefully, wondering if he suspected just how much she needed to get away from the hospital. 'But I think I'm well and truly ready for a move. What did you want to talk to me about? Not about Mr Foley, obviously.'

Dr Lucas did not generally seek her out for her professional opinion if he could help it, although a fair amount of fraternising had been inevitable. There had been a rivalry between them that she had preferred not to focus on over the last six months; she had tried to keep their interactions strictly professional, as had he.

'No. . .' he agreed, with that odd, lopsided smile that other female members of his medical team—as well as the cardiac team—seemed to find irresistibly attractive, if her observations over the past months were anything to go by.

Laurel looked away, her gaze sliding from his smiling mouth, his even white teeth, annoyed with herself because even in her anxiety about Mr Foley she could still find Jarrad Lucas attractive. She had not wanted to get embroiled in that way. . .even if she could presume the possibility of a reciprocal attraction—which she doubted.

He had given her no real indication that he found her attractive as a woman. . .yet there were vibes, which she did not think all arose from his animosity over the job that she had got with Dr Joshua Kapinsky—the job that he had wanted. She knew next to nothing about his private life, only that he was not married. And anyway, after the fracas with Max, she wanted to keep a firm hold on her emotions. . .

Dr Lucas took her elbow to shepherd her ahead of him into the elevator, as though he anticipated that she might want to get away. 'Come to the cafeteria with me,' he said. 'Have a coffee.'

'This is becoming more mysterious by the minute,' she said, jerking away from his touch. 'This being the first time you've ever invited me to have coffee with you.'

'Since we're both going to northern Canada, to the same place, we should perhaps have a little preliminary chat?' He put the suggestion as a question.

'Should we?' she countered, her fine dark eyebrows raised above wide blue eyes that now held a cynical gleam.

Being the only woman on a surgical team, in what was still very much a man's world, had made her wary of the motives of others. Fierce competition was the order of the day if one wanted to be accepted into surgery, which was acknowledged as the most macho and punishing service in that or any teaching hospital.

'I think so,' he said.

'Quite a coincidence,' she added, trying to go along with this pseudo friendship that he seemed to be initiating—that she did not trust one bit. 'That we should be going up north to Chalmers Bay at the same time. . . Although not really surprising, I suppose, when our jobs are both at an end now, plus the fact that the Northern Medical Development Corporation *does* have such an aggressive recruitment campaign going in this hospital, that they *do* want to forge strong links between the two places, to make us down here feel that we have a duty to help out in the wilds. . .and all that.'

She spoke flippantly, not bothering to disguise the sarcasm, and not yet sure how she really felt about the coincidence and what would be a close working relationship—much closer than they had enjoyed. . . or endured. . .at University Hospital.

'Mmm. . .maybe it's just that I can't bear to say goodbye to you for ever, Dr Laurel Harte.' He was smiling again. It was a cynical smile, mocking her, albeit compelling in its softening effect on his normally serious features. They both knew that his antipathy ran deep.

'That'll be the day!' she said.

The hospital cafeteria was huge—necessary to accommodate the hundreds of staff members, from the top medical staff to the floor cleaners, who ate there. Laurel served herself a mug of tea, then, having paid for it, chose two seats near the exit, shielded by a few tall potted plants. Whatever Dr Lucas had to say to her it would most likely be private, since it was not yet simply goodbye.

Having joined her, Jarrad drank half his mug of coffee without saying anything, lounging back easily in his chair, while she sipped the very welcome tea. As she sipped she diverted herself from the immediate scene by planning what she would do when she got back to her small, cosy apartment.

'What an unfortunate time to be leaving, now that this has happened to Mr Foley,' she said, voicing her underlying anxiety about the patient that was no longer hers. 'I...feel so awful...just going like this, when he's come to know me so well.'

The words dried up. She wished that Jarrad Lucas would not just sit there and look at her so intently, as though she were some sort of insect that he was looking at under a magnifying glass.

'Mmm...we can keep in touch. I'll go up to see him later,' he said. 'He's in good hands.'

There were two weeks to go before she left Gresham to fly, by various stages, to the Canadian Arctic to take up the temporary job for four months. Dr Lucas would go with her. After that, when the four months were over, she was not sure... There were several irons in the fire.

'What are you planning to do after Chalmers Bay?' Dr Lucas enquired casually, as though he were listening to her thoughts.

'Oh... I've already been interviewed for a job that I have every hope of getting,' she said, finding herself a little on the defensive about it. Not surprising really, with him. 'Junior staff surgeon.'

'Where?' he asked baldly.

'A small country hospital, not far from Gresham,' she said evasively, not caring to let him into her private life any more than she had to. When she had done that before, with someone else, disaster had struck. She had given Max all that she had had to give. 'I hope to be able to keep my apartment here in the city.'

Joshua, of course, would like to marry her. . .or so he had said. That was something she would definitely not tell Jarrad Lucas.

'I don't suppose you asked me here to make small talk about my future plans,' she said, feeling tense from their mutual wary scrutiny.

'No.' Her colleague produced a letter from the pocket of his lab coat and handed it to her. 'Read it,' he invited.

The letter was from the Northern Medical Development Corporation, whose headquarters were in Toronto. They recruited doctors on a temporary basis to work for several weeks or months in the Arctic, and one of the places they kept staffed in this way was a medical station in a remote community in the Northwest Territories—Chalmers Bay, on the edge of the Arctic Ocean.

That was where she would be going for four months, until she got her life sorted out on something like a permanent basis. And so, though unbeknown to her when she had applied, would Jarrad Lucas. While she felt disconcerted at the prospect he seemed merely amused, in a slightly predatory way, it seemed to her.

'Why are you showing me this?' she said tightly, handing him back the letter, having read it. A bitter anger was welling up inside her. It was beginning to appear that even in the far north she was not to be able to get away from the sexual politics, sometimes subtle, sometimes aggressively overt, that prevailed in the department of surgery at University Hospital.

'Just so that. . .this time. . .there won't be any mistake, any ambivalence about where we stand with each other professionally. No competition for the same job,' he said.

The letter, which was addressed to him, informed him that he was to be Medical Officer in Charge at Chalmers Bay Medical Station, and that she, Laurel, was to be his assistant. His superior age and experience, although he was only a few years older than she was, counted for a lot, apparently. As well they should in a place like that, she conceded unwillingly, where every bit of experience would be important.

'And I want to remind you,' he continued, his astute eyes holding her own, seeming to bore right into her soul, 'that in the north there won't be any sugar-daddy for you—no Joshua Kapinsky to protect you from the big, wide world, to give you preferential treatment.'

For quite a long time she had been the only female on the cardiac surgical team in the operating-rooms who had been unaware of Dr Kapinsky's penchant for getting any attractive nurse or female doctor in a tight, compromising corner, physically and emotionally, whenever he thought he could get away with it.

The nurses, apparently, tolerated him with a certain amusement, because he was a very admirable surgeon and good to work with, unlike some of the ranting prima donnas who passed through the portals of the vast operating suite. Laurel now felt a flush spreading over her cheeks.

'You would know all about that, wouldn't you, Laurel? Being his. . .er. . .girl. . . Or is it mistress?' Jarrad continued provokingly.

'How dare you be so. . .so unbearably rude?' Laurel would have got up to leave if she could have gathered together the necessary aplomb to make a good exit lumbered with two heavy bags.

She always felt surprised by the uncalled-for hostility of others, being an innocent herself. At least that was how she viewed herself. Dr Lucas had never spoken like this before. Now it was evident that her colleague was allowing his previously suppressed bitterness, which had probably festered for the last six months, to come to the fore.

'If you feel bitter because I got the senior residency with Dr Kapinsky—and I know you do—I refuse to take responsibility for that,' she forced herself to go on, goaded by anger. 'Since he is the head of Cardiac Services, I think he knew what he was doing when he chose me for the job instead of you.' She stopped then, her cheeks burning. How she had dreaded the possibility of this show-down that had been in the offing for weeks!

'You admitted at the time,' he countered, 'that you had no intention of doing cardiac surgery on a permanent basis, that you had plans to be a general surgeon in a small place. Whereas for me it would have been a very valuable further specialised training opportunity. I may very well do cardiac surgery as a specialty.'

Laurel's breath was coming in short, sharp gasps as the tension rose between them. At the time of accepting the job she had been aware that Dr Kapinsky had an eye for a pretty face, that he had a certain reputation, yet she had put it out of her mind at first, not entirely believing it. There had been plenty of other things to occupy her mind at the time.

Only later, when Joshua had begun to put pressure on her, had she tentatively and reluctantly admitted to herself that with herself and Jarrad more or less on par for the same job, her own attractiveness, her sex, might just have tipped the balance in her favour as far as Joshua had been concerned. The thought was sickening to her now.

'There wasn't much to choose between us, and you know it!' she said hotly, glaring at him across the expanse of the small table.

'That's a matter of opinion,' he said drily. 'He might have been looking for other things.'

'I've proved myself as much as you have!' she shot back.

'Maybe. Another reason I'm showing you the letter,' Jarrad went on relentlessly, 'is so that you can see it in writing. Then there won't be any misunderstanding between us. In the north we'll be working as a close-knit team—there won't be any nonsense in practice about who's junior, who's senior. Just so that you'll know—that's all.'

'You obviously enjoy making sure I know.'

Again he laughed, seeming genuinely amused at her outrage, lounging back in the chair that was scarcely big enough to hold his masculine frame.

As he lounged his lab coat pulled open to reveal the well-washed green scrub-suit taut over his muscular chest.

Unconsciously Laurel's eyes moved over him as she reluctantly felt the pull of his attraction. Angry with herself as much as with him, she lowered her eyes.

'This time I'm determined that we'll start off on the right foot. No rivalry, no competition—and no randy Josh to cloud the issue,' he said, suddenly leaning forward to put his elbows on the table and bring his face closer to her own. 'Were you. . .are you. . .his mistress, Laurel? Mmm?'

All Laurel could think of for a few seconds was that his mouth, chiselled and decisive, so close to her own, was very unlike the full, moist mouth of Joshua Kapinsky.

'You can tell me it's none of my business if you like. I've just always wanted to know.' He said the words softly. She could feel his breath on her skin as her cheeks became increasingly tinged with embarrassed colour. 'You see, I'm always intrigued to know how a beautiful young woman can sleep with a much older man. For some sort of material or social advantage? Professional?'

'Be quiet!' she snapped at him, inadvertently moving even closer, fearful that a passing colleague might hear the drift of their conversation. Apparently the velvet gloves were off now, the civilised veneer discarded.

'You're annoying me! And you're right in one thing. . .it is none of your business! I'll tell you anyway. No! I am not his mistress—I never have been. I got that job on merit. . .whatever *his* motives might have been apart from that. I. . .I didn't know about him in. . .that way.'

'No? You protest a little too much.'

'Do I?' Laurel parodied his sarcastic tone, glaring at him hotly, 'So do you! Like a baby who's had his candy taken away.'

As she sat stiffly in her chair, with the sharp edge of the small table between them digging into the soft flesh of her waist, she was glad that the clatter and bang of trays and cutlery around them drowned out their tense verbal exchange.

'So you're going to let it all out now, are you?' she added. 'I know you don't like me. Let me tell you—it's mutual!'

A few people glanced at them curiously as they passed the table on the way out of the cafeteria.

'You're telling me you were that naïve about Joshua?' Jarrad said incredulously, unmoved by her assertion of dislike. 'Josh Kapinsky has a reputation that goes back to his med school days. What was it. . . all of thirty years ago?'

'I wouldn't know. So what?' Laurel's throat felt tight

with emotion as other memories, nothing to do with Joshua Kapinsky, came flooding to the forefront of her mind. Memories of her young, dead husband, Max. Yes, she was naïve. She had been innocent then, too.

It had been her way then to bury herself in her work, where she was always in demand, to try to forget; it still was her way—destructive though it could become. Perhaps it had been her single-minded need to keep memories of Max at bay, her own guilt at his death, that had caused her to overlook the signs that the well-known and respected senior cardiac surgeon—her mentor—might have interests in her other than professional ones.

'I find that difficult to believe.' Jarrad's words interrupted her thoughts. 'That you didn't know. You're a very attractive woman. . . I've yet to meet a beautiful woman who didn't know it.'

'Perhaps your experience with women is limited, then,' she said. 'And believe what you like! I don't have to justify myself, or give an account of myself to you. There's been nothing unprofessional between myself and Dr Kapinsky.' That at least was true—during working hours.

'He's very discreet, so I've heard,' Jarrad drawled, keeping his voice low so that no one else could possibly hear, 'I can't believe that he would have passed you up. Even I have to admit that you're quite something. Just don't use it to gain any leverage while we're up north—with me or anyone else. It won't wash.'

'You arrogant. . .pompous. . .'

'"Bastard", I think, is the word that you're looking for,' he finished for her, his mouth quirking into a small, ironic smile. 'I seem to have reduced you to clichés. I've waited six months to have this out with you. Now that we're no longer officially employed in the department of surgery we can say what the hell we like to each other.

'And before you get up and stalk out in righteous indignation—' he leaned even closer, so that she could smell the delicate tang of a ginger and lime aftershave lotion that unaccountably made her head swim '—I want you to understand how I felt at being forced to play second fiddle in something that was essentially a repeat for me.'

'You don't have to spell it out,' she said. 'I've known from day one. How could I not know? And just about everyone else in the department! You certainly haven't made any secret of it.'

'I'm bitter—I don't mind admitting it,' he said. 'Yes, you're a good surgeon, a good doctor, but you were out of your league. You only stayed in it because of your personal relationship with Josh. When it's just you and me up north, when we're out of this place, we won't be playing any games, believe me! Don't you forget it!'

As Laurel brought up her right hand to hit the face that was in such close proximity to her own he swiftly caught it, so that anyone who had been watching them might have deduced that they were indulging in an emotional farewell.

Laurel felt tears stinging her eyes. 'I never was playing any games!' she spat out, feeling how inadequate those words were. The sophisticated riposte that should have come to her lips did not do so, because she felt numbed by the bitterness of his accusation.

Perhaps her mistake had been in keeping herself apart, in telling as few people as possible about Max. If she had been more open, it might have been obvious that she was not available as a potential mistress— least of all to her boss. What was the point of trying to defend herself now, of telling him that she found

Joshua physically and sexually unappealing? Yet she had let him kiss her, touch her...

Jarrad's hand was warm on hers as he held her with an iron grip. It was the first time he had touched her. 'Very charming,' he murmured as she stared at him speechless, with no hope of hiding the moisture that renewed itself in her wide, startled eyes. 'Perhaps now we know where we stand.'

'I think I hate you,' she whispered. The words were out before she could control the utterance. That was not what she had wanted to say.

He raised his eyebrows. 'That's a positive start!' he quipped.

Quickly she yanked her hand from his grasp and got to her feet, stumbling over a leg of her chair in her haste. 'If you react this way every time you don't get a job you expect to get, you're going to have a very hard life,' she retorted.

Not looking at him again, she picked up her two bags and walked out of the cafeteria, automatically taking the right door after running the gamut of a small group of chattering staff who were depositing empty trays on the moving conveyor belt near the exit.

She marched quickly, blinking back tears, looking straight ahead. She thought she heard Jarrad call her name, but she did not pause. Then she walked out of the staff cafeteria at University Hospital for the last time.

She located her car and thankfully threw the bags onto the back seat, then sat in the front and closed her eyes, leaning her head back against the headrest until the tumultuous churning of her emotions had subsided somewhat. Quarrels were hateful—particularly those that one did not initiate oneself. Now she let the tears ooze out unheeded.

Her ambivalence about Jarrad Lucas did not help; she wished she really did hate him.

His accusations touched her deeply as she thought about Dr Kapinsky. About a month ago, unexpectedly, Joshua had asked her to marry him. The proposal had brought her back to a reality from which she had been curiously distanced since the death of her husband—the reality that other men could look upon her as a potential wife, could find her attractive.

'I. . .I hadn't thought of marrying again,' she had stammered at the time, feeling herself recoiling involuntarily, both from the man and from the idea of being married to him—although he was not unattractive. 'At least. . .not for a very long time.' They had been in his house, where she had had lunch with him one weekend. All she had felt then was a kind of sick dismay. A sense of being flattered had come later—gradually.

'I'm very wealthy, as you can see,' Joshua had said baldly, spreading his arms wide to encompass the opulent furnishings of his very spacious home. 'I've come lately to be aware of. . .how shall I put it? Intimations of mortality?'

He was a stocky man of medium height, bullish and somewhat brash, very used to getting his own way. He had a slightly coarse, sensual attractiveness. As he had stood, squarely and solidly before her, he had obviously been determined not to let her quiet assertion sway him from his set course.

'I'm at the peak of my career now. . .there's nowhere else to go. I've put off marriage because I've been ninety-nine percent occupied with my career. Never been married. I could not have expected a woman to tolerate that. See?'

The proposal had been startling. That he was immensely rich was evident from their surroundings, where conspicuous consumption was tastefully subdued but nonetheless obvious. And, unlike many of his colleagues of the same age, who had been married more than once, the fact that he had never been married seemed to be in his favour.

'I'm speaking now because you're leaving,' Joshua had continued. 'I don't mind admitting that I don't want you to go. Yes, sure...I've played the field. Don't mind admitting that either. But I'm willing to change for you, Laurel. You're something damn special.'

His gruff, earnest manner, showing a total lack of awareness of the implicit insult in the magnanimous offer of himself, warts and all, might at some other time have been amusing if she had not been so taken aback. 'I want you as my soul mate, Laurel...as my hostess...I want to see you at the opposite end of the table when I entertain...and I entertain a lot. And, yes, damn it...I want you in my bed!'

'Well...I...don't know what to say.' She had struggled for words with burning cheeks, her professional admiration for him vying uncomfortably with a shrinking from the mental image of herself sharing a bed with him. For someone like herself, who had to struggle financially, he was a good prospect from a purely material point of view—had she been the opportunistic type. But she was not that way, and never would be.

'Now, I really like to see a woman who can blush.' Joshua had smiled at her discomfiture, staring at her openly with an undisguised sexual desire. 'That's pretty rare these days, and it sure does something to me, I can tell you!'

She remembered now how she had felt repelled that first time he had taken her in his arms and she had seen, with a sort of horrified fascination, the curling mat of grey hair on his chest that was revealed by his casual open shirt. She had almost expected to see a gold medallion nestled there; he was that kind of man—flamboyant, larger than life, just slightly in bad taste. That was one of the reasons why she was going north—to get away from him, to think.

When he had kissed her she had closed her eyes tightly, pretending that he was someone else, a movie star. . .anyone. Without any apparent volition on her part, the dark, lean and cynical face of Jarrad Lucas had floated before her mind's eye and remained there for the duration of the kiss, tantalisingly. At the end of it, Joshua had looked gratified, triumphant. She had not yet given him an answer, had somehow put him off.

The sound of a car engine starting up near her jolted her back to the present and the concrete jungle of the hospital car park, where a bright spring sunshine, still lacking in warmth after the hard winter, gleamed on the tops of dusty cars.

Decisively Laurel got out of the car, calmer now, drawing her warm coat around her. She could not leave the hospital without seeing Mr Foley once again; she had become very fond of him, had forged links with his family. Over the next two weeks she would keep in touch by telephone to see how he was doing.

She walked briskly through the vast lobby of the Edith Cavell Wing, up two flights of stairs to the intensive care unit where Mr Foley had been transferred.

'He's pretty good,' the nurse said to Laurel as she enquired about Mr Foley. 'He's still in the X-ray department at the moment, having an angiogram. Dr Kapinsky's talking about maybe doing the bypass this evening, depending on what they find.'

Laurel made her way quickly to the X-ray department, not wanting to go now without seeing Mr Foley, even though she had no desire to see Joshua. Without a doubt he would find ways to see her in the two weeks that she had left before going up north.

The angiogram had obviously been completed by the time she got to X-Ray. Quickly passing by the chief radiologist's office and glancing through the open door, she could see the radiologist and Joshua engrossed in looking at the films that were up on the lighted display units on the wall. Laurel would have liked to look at the films too, but did not want to intrude now that she was no longer officially on staff. The doctors did not see her.

A nurse told her that Mr Foley was in one of the diagnostic rooms nearby. She had not expected to encounter Jarrad Lucas again, yet as she went through the doorway of the room she saw that he was there, standing by the stretcher on which Mr Foley lay, and she stopped abruptly.

'Come in, Dr Harte,' Jarrad said, having spotted her immediately and before she could retreat. The desire to do so must have been clearly on her face. 'I'm not going to attack.'

Advancing warily, she could see that Jarrad had a hand covering one of Mr Foley's hands that lay inert on top of the sheet. With mixed emotions she registered that he was capable of tenderness, after all. To be fair, he was always very good with patients.

Mr Foley still had the tube in his mouth, although he was now breathing spontaneously, and his colour was good. Sympathy for him flooded over Laurel as she walked to the other side of the stretcher and touched his hand with hers, glad that he felt warm, alive. Just then he opened his eyes and recognised her.

She smiled and gave the thumbs-up sign, fighting to keep obvious signs of emotion at bay as she witnessed his pathetic attempt to smile at her with the tube filling his mouth. She made a show of checking the monitors to which he was attached, knowing that he could not speak to her either. Probably she would never see Mr Foley again after this visit.

'This your last day, Dr Harte?' The nurse, who had come in with her, spoke to her quietly.

'Yes.'

'Dr Kapinsky's going to really miss you,' the nurse said. 'You're his right-hand woman.'

Jarrad Lucas looked at her again, searchingly.

In Laurel's heightened emotional state, after their earlier show-down, the nurse's words seemed to have a greater significance than she would otherwise have supposed—even a snide connotation. Was it possible that everyone but she herself had clearly seen her senior colleague's intentions in relation to her?

The thought was humiliating. She made a non-committal murmur.

When Mr Foley's eyelids fluttered shut she said a silent goodbye to him and left.

CHAPTER TWO

WAKING up to a moaning wind in the dim light of morning, Laurel wondered momentarily where she was. Scenes of Gresham were never far from her mind.

Then she stretched luxuriously in the comfortable bed under the warm duvet, realising that it was a Saturday in Chalmers Bay, Northwest Territories, and that she had a whole day off.

A shade covered the small window of her bedroom. It was early summer down south, late spring here; soon there would be sunlight twenty-four hours a day. They were well above the Arctic Circle, on the Arctic Ocean where it flowed from west to east along Coronation Gulf.

In the summer, huge supply barges would make the long journey up the MacKenzie River to the Arctic Ocean, from Great Slave Lake far to the south, bringing precious and much needed heavy supplies to many small, isolated communities along the top of the continent where no roads or railways came. The supply season was short; all too soon the cold winds of an early autumn would blow away the blessed summer heat from the tundra, and winter would descend again with all its fury and bleakness.

She and Jarrad Lucas had already been at the medical station for four weeks. The two of them shared a small, free-standing medical staff annexe that was connected to the main clinical area of the medical station proper by a covered way that kept the elements from intruding too much in their professional comings and goings.

The oddity of actually living with Jarrad, who had hitherto seemed a rather prickly and definitely enigmatic colleague, was giving way to a somewhat grudging acceptance on her part of his continual presence. Surprisingly, their latent animosity had not again come to the surface in an outburst such as the one they had shared in Gresham.

Off duty they were carefully polite to each other; on duty they had been far too busy learning and doing, making a professional shifting of gears.

Jarrad was on call today, while she had the day off, then the positions would be reversed tomorrow. Because there were only the two of them, plus two long-term permanent nurses at the medical station, they did not trespass on what might be considered the other's territory. His designated title of chief had not yet had any practical significance.

Laurel heard the telephone ring in the annexe sitting-room and was instantly alert, even though the call would be taken by Jarrad.

Although they were living in a very remote place, the communications systems were superb, thanks to the use of satellites. Perhaps there was an emergency. All calls came through initially to the nurse in charge, Bonnie Mae, in her own personal quarters over the weekend. Laurel sighed, knowing that she might as well get up.

'Ah. . . Laurel, I'm glad you're up. It saves me from having to shake you awake. Coffee? You look as though you could use some.' Jarrad came out of the kitchen carrying a mug of coffee just as she emerged into their shared sitting-room, wearing her warm wool dressing-gown and sheepskin slippers. He was casually dressed in jeans and a checked shirt.

Laurel had refused on principle to brush her tangled hair, was determined that she would live in the annexe just as she would live in her own apartment—relaxed and casual. Yet now she thought she could detect an implied criticism in Jarrad's remark, and saw his cool regard moving over her assessingly from head to toe.

Very deliberately she returned the assessment, having to concede again, grudgingly, that he looked very good in jeans. Although lean, he was muscular, fit, seeming to hold himself ready for action at a moment's notice.

'I'd love some coffee. Are you going to pour it for me?' she asked, hoping to deflect his probing, very perceptive assessment of her cosily clad body to something else. 'And why would you have to shake me awake?'

'That call, which you must have heard, was from the redoubtable Bonnie Mae. There's a guy at one of the gold mines around here...the Black Lake mine, I think she said...who's being flown in here with lower abdominal pain. Sounds like an incarcerated hernia to me—at least, he's got a lump which can't be reduced.'

As Jarrad spoke he moved back into the kitchen and she followed him. 'He suspected he had a hernia, but didn't tell anyone about it because he could always push it back before. We should do something about it before it becomes a strangulated hernia—which it may well be by the time we get to see him. I'd like your opinion about whether we should operate on him here, or have him flown out on the next available plane to Yellowknife.'

He poured her a mug of coffee, turning his back to her to do it, and Laurel found herself openly staring at him, at his smooth dark hair and angular profile. At other times she felt that she had to keep a veil over her expression, she was not sure exactly why. He could be trouble for her, she sensed that.

'So much for your day off,' he said. He turned quickly and caught her unawares, saw her looking at him as any woman might look at an attractive man.

As she reached forward to take the coffee she lowered her eyes, aware of a stillness between them. When she looked at him again, there was a perceptiveness in his astute grey eyes, an awareness of her as a woman rather than as a colleague, that made her suddenly vulnerable; it was fleeting, then gone.

'Yes. . .that at least doesn't change,' she said quickly. 'If we have to operate, do you want me to do the surgery?'

'If you prefer it,' he said softly. 'Then I'll give the anaesthetic. We ought to give him a general anaesthetic, I think—if we decide to do it at all.'

'Yes, I would prefer to do the surgery. . .if you don't mind.' She looked away again, feeling tense.

'No. . .I don't.' He eyed her perceptively, aware of her discomfiture. 'You don't have to behave as though you were walking around on eggshells, Laurel.'

'Don't I? You are the chief, after all. Which you took great care to inform me about. . .put me very firmly in my place—whatever you perceive that to be.'

'I'm not about to pull rank. We've done surprisingly well so far, so don't let's spoil it. Okay?'

Laurel moved past him. She began to break eggs carefully into a bowl for scrambled eggs. 'How long before they get here?'

'About three-quarters of an hour at the earliest, Bonnie Mae said. They're coming in a light plane—a Cessna, I believe—from the mine's own airstrip, then being met here by the Royal Canadian Mounted Police. They'll bring him here in their pick-up truck ambulance. If we decide not to operate, we'll contact the airstrip here to hold the next big plane out to Yellowknife, provided that one comes fairly soon.

Bonnie Mae's organising all that.'

Yellowknife was the capital of the Northwest Territories, which had a hospital. It was here that most of the doctors who covered the vast and sparsely populated territories worked. She and Jarrad had passed through it on their way up north, had changed planes there. It was a very long way to the south—now seeming impossibly remote from them.

'It's quite a long time since I've done a routine hernia repair,' she admitted. 'It's one of those things once learnt, never forgotten, I expect.' She turned to look at him briefly as she cooked the eggs. 'And if it turns out to be more than routine, it will be that much more of a challenge. I'm actually looking forward to it.'

Not least of all to show him again that she was more than capable of turning her hand to anything, as she had been doing over the past month, she told herself silently. She was getting a gradual sense that he was suitably impressed. Likewise, she was impressed with him. But then, she always had been. Only, now she was more impressed.

'Mmm. I'm sure you'll be great,' he said, without inflexion.

Laurel then dismissed the impending operation from her mind for the time being. 'Have you eaten?' she asked.

'Yes, thanks. I'll get changed into my scrub suit.' He turned away.

Laurel felt herself relax. What had got into her this morning, to make her feel so tense, on edge, she had no idea. Perhaps it was that on other weekends they had been out of the annexe really early, busy with emergencies, not actually being together much with time to spare in the mornings at breakfast. Maybe, too, she was getting fed up with not having an uninterrupted day off. It was very easy to get overtired, burnt out.

'By the way,' Jarrad said casually, pausing on the way to his room, 'I picked up the mail from the post office this morning. There are several letters for you.' He indicated a small pile of letters on their dining-table.

'There's also one addressed to a Mrs Max Freer, care of the medical station staff annexe. Would that be you, by any chance?' There was an odd expression on his face when she looked at him—curious, mystified and watchful. 'I knew a Max Freer...a Dr Max Freer.'

'Yes,' she said quietly, 'I expect it was the same one...if you knew him in Gresham. I was his wife.' She had no idea who would be writing to her using that name, since she had long ago stopped using it, had always used her maiden name for professional purposes.

'You!' His voice was soft, incredulous as he moved back into the centre of the room. 'You...were married to Max Freer?' He was frowning, looking at her oddly again, as though there was no earthly possibility that she could have been married to Max Freer.

'Is that so odd?' she countered, trying not to be too defensive. 'You've often seemed to make it obvious to me that you don't consider me like other women—"normal" women, who do things like get married, run a home, have babies.'

'So you were married to him?' he repeated.

'Yes...I was. I had no idea you knew him.' The tenseness was back.

'I...' His words were drowned out by the sound of the telephone ringing in his room. Abruptly he left her to answer it.

Laurel took the opportunity to go to her own room

with her letters—hastily—taking a plate of scrambled eggs and toast with her. There was no way that she was going to discuss her private life with Jarrad; it was none of his business. Besides, she found his incredulity insulting.

There were two letters from Joshua, with his printed letterhead on the envelope, which Jarrad must obviously have noticed. Perhaps Joshua would be repeating his offer of marriage...twice. She smiled to herself wryly. She would put off reading them all until later. She hoped that Josh would give her the latest update on Mr Foley, who had survived the operation and been discharged home some time ago.

The letter with her married name on it was from the bank that had given her a mortgage to buy her apartment. The sight of it afforded her a small pang of anxiety—especially as she had given money to her actress sister Lucy before her departure, and was subsequently somewhat short herself. Lucy was chronically under-employed and relied on frequent help.

How easy the possibility of marrying Joshua seemed at times—how easy to accept the financial security that he had to offer. How easy...after the roller coaster life she had experienced being married to Max.

Automatically she ate her breakfast, had a quick shower and dressed in a scrub suit, her mind going over the procedure for a routine incarcerated hernia.

If an abdominal hernia could not be pushed back into the abdominal cavity, a loop of bowel which protruded into the hernia sac could become twisted and constitute a surgical emergency—a strangulated hernia. In that case, the blood supply to the piece of herniated bowel could be cut off and the bowel become gangrenous.

If that had happened, they would definitely have to operate here in Chalmers Bay, rather than risk putting the man on a long flight to the hospital in Yellowknife.

They tried not to have in-patients here, if they could possibly avoid it, because there were not enough staff members to take care of them; all hands were needed for the on-going day to day work of the medical station, for the emergencies and the ever-present possibility of accidents and severe trauma.

Jarrad knocked at her bedroom door. 'I'm going over there, Laurel,' he informed her through the door. Quickly she opened it. 'Bonnie Mae would like to go over your preferred sutures with you before the patient gets here. She's called in Skip to scrub for you.'

'Sure. I'll be over there in a couple of minutes. You go ahead,' she answered him.

While she could still hear his receding footsteps on the wooden floor of the covered way leading to the medical station she began to apply a subtle make-up quickly and expertly to her face and added a dab of perfume behind each ear.

No one could say that she played down her femininity, even if she was in a job that was generally considered reserved largely for men, she thought with satisfaction as she contemplated her appearance in her bathroom mirror. Her full, shapely lips, tinged with a little added red, smiled back at her. Then she turned away, dismissing everything from her mind but the job in hand.

Their patient was forty years old, a short, stocky miner who was in a lot of pain and complaining of nausea. The RCMP had lost no time in getting him from the airstrip to the medical station in their ambulance. The operating-room was ready for the operation, with Skip, the operating-room technician, a local Inuit man, scrubbed and waiting with all his sterile equipment set up, and Bonnie Mae, the registered nurse, standing by.

The two doctors examined their patient, Mr Berny

Allett, taking turns to do what was necessary. It was very obvious that the preliminary diagnosis made by the paramedic personnel at the gold mine was correct. The incipient vomiting was not a good sign.

'Looks like he's obstructed,' Jarrad commented, observing Laurel's hands as they moved gently over Mr Allett's abdomen, where the obvious lump in his right groin was very tender and could not be reduced. He winced and groaned every time she touched it.

'Mmm,' she agreed. 'When did you last eat, Mr Allett?'

'Not since early yesterday,' he replied with effort. 'And not much at that.'

'Good.'

'The hernia is what we call "strangulated",' Jarrad informed him. 'Although we appear to have just caught it in time. . .so I don't think we'll have to remove any of the bowel. But we won't know until we make an incision and have a look at it, which we're going to do right away.'

'OK,' he agreed resignedly. 'This pain is killing me.'

Things moved quickly after that. Bonnie Mae, who had everything highly organised, wheeled the stretcher into the operating-room with Jarrad's help.

Something in Mr Allett's favour was that he was a good anaesthetic risk—he did not smoke or drink, had no history of heart or lung problems himself or in his family, had no chronic illnesses and appeared to be fit and well apart from the hernia.

Laurel went to the scrub sinks that were situated just outside the main operating-room door in the compact clinic area, where she began to soap her hands and arms prior to putting on her sterile surgical gown and gloves. She was very mindful—as no doubt they all were—that before the Northern Medical Development Corporation had arranged such a good set-up in

Chalmers Bay, sick people like Mr Allett would have had to wait to be flown out to the city on the next available commercial flight. Some patients would have died en route, or before departure.

Jarrad came back out of the main operating-room and sauntered over to her. 'Are you still happy to do the operation?' he queried, his expression neutral as he lounged casually against the sinks.

'Yes.' She smiled at him warmly, very confident now in her abilities, only sorry that he could not see her luscious red mouth because of the enveloping face mask that she wore. Undoubtedly, though, he could smell her very expensive French perfume, because he leaned closer, inhaling deeply.

'I won't hesitate to ask your advice if I need it. . . chief,' she said. 'And I wouldn't be a bit surprised if Skip could do the operation himself—or Bonnie Mae. They have to be pretty versatile up here. So you can all chip in with your advice.'

'OK, ma'am. Anything you say!'

'You could have fooled me!' she said.

'Mmm. . .that perfume could be addictive,' he murmured appreciatively, breathing deeply. Coming very close to her, pulling down his face mask so that she could feel his warm breath on the exposed skin at the back of her neck, he breathed in again. 'You should use that more often,' he added huskily.

Then, before she could guess what he might do, he placed his lips on her bare skin, sending an involuntary shiver of delight through her that he could not fail to observe.

When her face reddened, he laughed softly. 'That will teach you not to mess with me, Dr Laurel Harte. Not to get too mouthy.' She knew he was teasing. 'I like to see you blush. . .it's one of the few indications you give that you're human. . .and a woman.'

Although he said it jokingly, she sensed that he meant every word of it.

'That's funny,' she said, wanting to get back at him, 'Joshua liked it too. Now go away!' She flicked water at him from her wet hands, furious at her own reaction. 'And I don't suppose you're the world's greatest lover, Dr Lucas,' she dared to add, knowing she was lying, spurred by the niggling annoyance of his teasing assault on her womanhood.

It was amazing in itself that they had got to a stage of being sufficiently relaxed with each other to tease. They were indulging in the verbal sparring that was so common in every operating-room, that served to defuse tension. It seemed even more necessary here, where there were only the two of them, forced to rely on each other. With them, there were other, underlying motivations too, which Laurel did not care to analyse then.

'If that's a challenge, perhaps I'll take you up on it some time,' was all he said, before disappearing into the room to start the anaesthetic. Laurel continued to soap her arms energetically, waiting for the colour to subside from her face, and wondering at the gradual, unpredictable changes in their relationship.

What she did know was that after her experience of being married to Max something in her had died—a kind of sweet innocence, an optimism for the future, that would perhaps never be resurrected. She also knew that Jarrad's rare flirtatious humour served to mask his mistrust. She sighed, giving her hands and arms a final rinse under the running water.

The operation went smoothly, with Laurel giving her total concentration to it, helped by Skip who was quietly efficient.

'That's a relief,' Jarrad commented from his position at the head of the operating-table when Laurel released the piece of herniated bowel that had become twisted and thus strangulated. 'It's not beyond redemption.'

As soon as the pressure was released, they could see that the blood supply was being restored again as they watched.

'Yes,' Laurel agreed, with a slight laugh of relief. 'I didn't really fancy doing a gut resection today.'

Nonetheless, they would have to watch Mr Allett closely for several days, to make sure that his bowel was working as it should be. He would need a nasogastric tube in place, through which he could receive fluids, as well as having intravenous fluid until it was obvious that he could digest oral fluids and then a light diet. Once the crisis was over he would have to be flown down to the city for the recovery period and some possible follow-up tests.

'He won't be able to work in the mine again for several weeks,' Jarrad said, thinking aloud. 'And probably won't be able to do any sort of really heavy work again. I guess you'll have to fly down with him and his wife, Bonnie Mae. . .we can't risk letting him go unaccompanied on such a long flight.'

'Yep. I'm resigned to that,' Bonnie Mae said. 'I can go on a mad shopping spree, and all!'

Beside the operating-room was a small recovery room, into which their patient was wheeled on the stretcher when the operation was over and he had regained consciousness. The two doctors stood beside him while Bonnie Mae connected up the monitors that would automatically record his heart rate, his blood pressure, his temperature and his circulating oxygen. They kept an oxygen mask on his face.

'We'll take turns staying with him,' Jarrad stated. 'I'll do the first few hours, since I gave the anaesthetic—if that's OK with you, Laurel? And you, Bonnie? What about the afternoon shift?'

'Sure. You can do the first part of the night, Doc,' Bonnie Mae said to Laurel. 'Then I'll get Nuna, the nursing aide, to come in from the village to do the early morning hours...that will give us a chance to get a bit of sleep.'

'That sounds good,' Laurel commented. 'And I'll relieve you, Jarrad, in a couple of hours.'

'Just relieve me for lunch, since it's your day off, then I'll go back.'

'All right. I'll order lunch from the central kitchen for you.' Laurel took the patient's chart and began to write up her notes on the operating procedure while it was still fresh in her mind.

Back in the annexe kitchen she made herself lunch, now ravenously hungry again after the activity.

They also had a central kitchen for the medical station, where a permanent cook, Joe Fletcher, would prepare and deliver meals to order. He also did the same for the Royal Canadian Mounted Police, otherwise known as the RCMP, and for several other official outfits in the community, managing to keep himself extremely busy.

'Will do!' Joe said, when she telephoned him to order a lunch for Jarrad later. 'It's pot luck today... caribou meat and frozen fiddle heads.'

'Fiddle heads?' she queried.

'Yes, they're the curled tops of new fern shoots—very edible.'

'I don't believe you,' she laughed.

'You wait and see,' he said.

When Jarrad came back to the annexe she was reading through her mail in the sitting-room, having had a short, much needed, sleep. Joshua wrote witty, amusing letters, containing anecdotes about staff members with whom she was very familiar and showing a surprising insight that she had not known he possessed. She found herself warming to his efforts on her behalf.

Before Jarrad had come in she had been musing again on how easy it would be to say yes to Joshua, to give him what he wanted.

But I don't love him. . .don't feel for him in the right way, a small, persistent voice protested at the back of her mind.

'Oh, hi!' she said brightly. 'I was just thinking of coming over there to relieve you.'

'Hi!' Jarrad said, somewhat brusquely, as he entered the room, taking in the sight of her smiling over her letter. There was no sign of his earlier flippant mood when she had flicked water at him. The recollection of it did not exactly make for easy camaraderie right now.

'Don't bother to go over there yet,' he said. 'Bonnie Mae's taken over for a while,' he added as she made to get up. 'Everything's fine.'

'Good. Actually, I really wanted to get out of the room before you see the caribou meat and fiddle heads that you have for lunch,' she quipped.

'What?' he said, in mock horror, some of his previous good humour returning.

'That's what Joe said.' She smiled, relaxing back in her chair again. 'Never mind!'

'That's a euphemism for steak and fries, I hope,' he said. He looked pale and tired. 'Is that a letter from old Josh?' he added, looking pointedly at the letter she was holding. 'I guess he's still stanching blood and saving lives, driving his Cadillac and collecting women, hmm? What does he have to say? You don't have to tell me anything personal, of course.'

There was an edge of sarcasm in his voice as he threw himself down in a chair, stretched out his long legs and closed his eyes.

'Well. . .' She hesitated, then dared to say

it. 'He wants to marry me, actually.'

Slowly he opened his eyes and lifted up his head to look at her. For a long moment his gaze held hers while he said nothing. 'Like hell he does!' he said at last, his lips curling in a cynical smile. 'And what do you have to say to that?'

'I...haven't decided yet.'

'No? Surely you'll take him up on it? You sure wouldn't need to operate on strangulated hernias in a place like Chalmers Bay.' The cynicism was so obvious now that she flinched inwardly.

'Maybe I will take him up on it,' she said lightly. 'I just thought I would dangle him on a string for a while, make him wait, seeing that I'm such a calculating person.' She stood up. 'Isn't that what you think... still...Dr Lucas?'

He stood up too, facing her down. 'Yeah...that just about sums it up.'

Her attempt at nonchalance to hide the underlying antagonism had not come off, so it was with relief that she saw Joe Fletcher, the cook, coming in from the covered way.

'Hi there!' he said, giving Laurel a conspiratorial wink over the tray that he was carrying. 'Here's your lunch, Dr Lucas. Steak and fries. All the men like that. Women like pasta and salad. Right?' He was a rangy, thin man, with a somewhat cadaverous face that was permanently set in deep, humorous lines.

'You're right, Joe,' she said, smiling back.

'That's great, Joe.' Jarrad took the tray from him. 'Thanks.'

It was amazing how courteous he could be to some people, Laurel observed, gathering up her letters to leave, deciding to go over anyway to see if Bonnie Mae wanted a break for lunch.

Since working on the cardiac team at Gresham she

had developed a thick skin, yet sometimes it was not quite thick enough—even though she had brought this on herself. Now she wanted to get away.

'Wait. . .' Jarrad detained her. 'You said this morning that you had been married to Max Freer.'

'Yes.'

'That's strange,' he said, 'because. . .I thought he was married to someone else.' He was looking at her broodingly, standing squarely in front of her, his hands in the pockets of his lab coat. 'Perhaps we're not talking about the same Max Freer—although I rather suspect that we are.'

'What do you mean?' she asked, a feeling of cold apprehension giving her the sense of being momentarily suspended in time.

'I was at a medical conference in the States, in Cleveland, about two and a half years ago,' he said slowly, his astute eyes fixed on her face. 'Max was there. . .with a woman he introduced as his wife. It wasn't you, obviously.'

Laurel ran her tongue over her dry lips, lowering her eyes from his intent, observant regard. 'No,' she agreed at last. 'I remember that meeting. I couldn't go with him. I don't think he asked me anyway. What was her name. . .the woman?'

Strangely she felt calm, yet slightly physically sick at the same time. What did it matter anyway? she asked herself silently. She hadn't loved Max at that point; it had been all over between them, even if they had still been legally married. It had been enlightening to discover that once you stopped loving someone you were free again, even if you could still feel pain, could mourn.

A liberation of sorts had come to her with that realisation, even though Max's casual philandering had delivered constant blows to her self-esteem. That was perhaps why Joshua Kapinsky's amorous interest in her had not seemed real at first, she saw now, with a new insight.

'He introduced her as Renate,' Jarrad said, his well-modulated, deep drawl adding a caressing note to the unusual name, so that Laurel could immediately conjure up the image of the woman, whom she had met once or twice.

'I see.' Laurel spoke automatically, thinking back. 'She was a research assistant, I believe. They had been working on some sort of project together...'

Her voice trailed off. Max had had other women that she had known about; it had been almost inevitable, given the amount of time that she and Max had been forced to spend apart. So what did one more matter? They had been like strangers in the end.

'Max always expected me to understand when he had to work or study, when he was not available to me,' she went on, finding a rare relief in unburdening herself. 'Then he expected me to be always available to him when he needed me...'

It was not in her nature to complain, when no one but herself had been responsible for the situation that she had found herself in, so she paused, doubting that he wanted to hear her troubles.

She was aware of Jarrad touching her hand, the warmth of his fingers on her bare skin startling her back to the here and now.

'Laurel...I had no idea earlier that you were his wife...no idea at all. I heard that you'd been married...I guess I assumed that you were divorced. Perhaps I shouldn't have told you about Renate. Maybe you didn't want to know.' He spoke evenly, yet the vibes were back.

She jerked away from him, flashing him a quick glance, feeling vulnerable before his searching scrutiny.

'It doesn't matter. In fact, you've done me a favour.' Her tone was brittle. 'I've been castigating myself with guilt since his death in that accident—guilt that I wasn't a proper wife to him, that I didn't love him, or even like him in the last year or so of our marriage. Now I don't have to feel guilty, do I?' she challenged, turning to face him, holding her head up. 'Knowing that he had Renate.'

'Maybe not,' he said.

'It's all in the past now. . .I want to put it behind me.'

'But you haven't succeeded yet, have you, Laurel?' he said, with shrewd accuracy, his voice soft. 'Exactly when was the accident?'

'Just a little more than two years ago.' Her voice quavered.

'For God's sake, Laurel, why the hell did none of us know at University Hospital about you and Max? It might have explained a few things. Why so secretive?'

'We spent so little time together. I didn't want anyone feeling sorry for me, asking me personal questions. That's why I kept my maiden name too.'

In spite of her denial that his revelation mattered, she found herself trembling, almost imperceptibly. Jarrad noticed. His handsome, lean face was enigmatic as he looked down into her eyes. Very slowly, as their eyes locked, he put his hands on her shoulders, causing her to stiffen. In his expression she read a veiled sympathy. A question was there also, one that she could not read. . .

'Laurel. . .you poor kid.' He murmured the words so that she could scarcely hear them.

'Don't pity me,' she ordered, straining away from him nervously as he held her firmly in place with his strong hands, so that her head was tilted back and her hair hung away from her shoulders in a tumbled mass.

They seemed to be in a timeless moment, in a strange battle of wills. Then she saw in his eyes an overt sexual awareness, a desire, a softness...and her heart began a deep, accelerated pounding.

'I don't pity you,' he said. His hand moved to her face, moulding her cheek warmly, his thumb moving caressingly over her parted lips. She felt mesmerised by his unexpected touch. 'Do you want to talk about it some more? Mmm? It might help. Tell me how you got involved with him.'

'I...we met when we were both medical students,' she said, speaking quickly, trying not to be so terribly affected by the warm feel of his fingers on her face, needy as she was for such warmth, for a male touch that was unconditional. After all, she didn't really like Jarrad Lucas, she told herself, and she willed herself to concentrate on that dislike. She did not think to move away from him, though.

'We had—er—come to know each other really well through a new mentor program that had been set up in the medical school, which occasionally put junior medical students with more senior students for teaching purposes on an individual basis.'

'He must have been quite a bit older than you,' Jarrad murmured, moving his hand down again to rest on her shoulder.

'Yes...well, two years older. He was my mentor. I guess I sort of idolised him...almost from the first moment. The program forced us to be together quite a lot. In other circumstances we...might not have come into contact. Certainly I would not have supposed that he would be interested in me...'

'Why not?' Jarrad said softly, persistently.

'When you're at the age I was...' She sought for words, only too aware of the weight of his hands on her shoulders. 'A...a two-year gap between two people, especially in medical school, is an awfully big one.'

'Yeah,' Jarrad agreed, in the understated, cynical way that he sometimes had.

'I guess it wasn't surprising that I fell in love with him,' she whispered, her head bent. 'He seemed so. . . sophisticated, all-knowing, so ready to share his superior knowledge with me. I guess I was really flattered at the time. And. . .he seemed interested in me.'

What she couldn't tell Jarrad was that she had been very inexperienced with men. Max had been undeniably good looking, very masculine. Other girls in her group had envied her, so they had said. Max had seemed equally smitten.

'Seemed?' Jarrad murmured. 'It's pretty obvious that he *was* interested in you. The guy married you.'

'Yes. . .' she said absently, thinking back now with a kind of sad detachment. Laurel knew that she was attractive—beautiful, even, judging by the reactions she got from men—but she had never been the sort of woman to exploit her appearance in any deliberate way, would not have known how.

'I'm still listening,' Jarrad reminded her.

'We decided to marry just after he graduated from medical school,' she continued.

'Before he'd done his internship year?' he asked incredulously. 'That was asking for trouble. And you had two more years of medical school.'

'Yes. . .' she said again. It had been foolish, the whole thing. After a short honeymoon, they had quickly returned to work.

'During the next year,' she went on, 'we spent more time apart than we did together. Much of the time Max slept at the hospital to be on call at a moment's notice. . . Anyway, you know all about that sort of life. I concentrated on studying for my finals. When we did meet, we tried to make up for lost time...not very successfully.'

Laurel looked up at Jarrad then. 'You can guess the rest. I suppose we were doomed from the beginning,' she said. 'I don't want to talk about it any more now.'

When he brought his head down slowly, to place his cheek against hers, she held her breath, immobilised. Then, as she stood in shocked silence, he was kissing her neck, her ear, her temple, gently but insistently, as though he was willing her to respond to him, drawing her out like a flower to the sunlight.

When his lips covered hers, a small, involuntary cry formed itself in her throat, muffled; it was part protest, part fear, and part a longing to consent to pleasure, to give herself permission...because it was a pleasure.

They clung to each other with a controlled desperation, as though there was an unspoken mutual fear that the telephone would ring at any moment—as it had done so many times before for them—with a call to duty. For a month now they had been together the tension building, coming inexorably to this explosion of emotion...

'Laurel... Laurel...' Jarrad murmured against her ear, his voice unsteady. 'That's a beautiful name... evergreen...enduring...'

'Mmm...' Laurel felt that she might faint from the swift flood of longing that unaccountably swept through her at the husky rendering of her name, a longing more powerful than she had ever experienced before in her life.

'Who decided on that name for you?' he persisted, his lips touching the sensitised lobe of her ear.

'My...English grandmother,' she whispered.

'Sensible woman...'

As the word 'sensible' seemed to reverberate in the air Laurel drew back from Jarrad, pulling out of his arms.

They stood looking at each other, the atmosphere charged with something different now, something other than the customary tension of a professional rivalry tempered by a teasing relationship. As well, his unspoken acknowledgement of desire for her had somehow equalled their relationship as no amount of professional interaction could do, and she felt a sobering vindication.

'I always thought I didn't like you. . .' she murmured at last.

Jarrad raised his eyebrows in pretended surprise. 'I thought it was hate!' he said. 'Anything less is quite an admission, coming from you, Laurel.'

'You can't pretend that there's any love lost on your part.'

'I prefer not to comment on that,' he said, breaking eye contact and running a hand through his hair.

'Now that you know just about all there is to know about my personal life, perhaps you'll tell me why you're so. . .uptight about women in the medical profession. An unhappy love affair, perhaps?' She asked the probing question with more aplomb than she felt, feeling the urge to know something about this enigmatic man who kept very much to himself, yet who was obviously capable of a tender understanding.

'I think we've had enough revelations for now,' he said tensely. By the way his lips tightened, Laurel could tell that she had, almost inadvertently, perhaps, stumbled on something of the truth. Without another word he prepared to eat his belated lunch, while she escaped—coward that she was—over to the medical station.

At eleven o'clock that night Laurel sat near the bed of Mr Berny Allett, writing up her notes on his condition and waiting for the nursing aide to relieve her so that she could go to bed. Mr Allett was sleeping, snoring actually, having had a sedative by injection about an hour and a half earlier.

Laurel smiled tiredly to herself, relieved that he seemed to be recovering well, that no really major surgery had been necessary with him. What they had to watch out for now was that he did not get a paralysis of the bowel. Other than that everything would return to normal functioning. Accordingly, they had left the naso-gastric tube in place so that he could be given fluids orally and so that his stomach contents could be aspirated with a syringe if necessary. The intravenous drip was still in place also.

They had moved him into a proper bed early in the evening so that they could shift him from the recovery room to the small ward area that held several other beds, all empty at the moment. She and Jarrad, in consultation with Bonnie Mae, had decided that Mr Allett would be flown out to the city on Tuesday, three days from now, when he should be on the mend.

There would be a commercial flight arriving at twelve noon in Chalmers Bay, which would take off again at one o'clock. Bonnie Mae would go with him and his wife, and would be back on the Thursday, late.

Laurel allowed herself to relax in her chair and deliberately think about what had happened between herself and Jarrad earlier. She put her head in her hands, closing her tired eyes and pressing her fingers against the lids, trying to calm her chaotic emotions.

Up to now she had tried to force it out of her mind while she concentrated on Mr Allett's condition. Feeling a certain sense of shock now, it seemed utterly incredible that such contact had happened with comparative ease between them. . .that it had happened at all. There was an air of unreality about all of it.

CHAPTER THREE

TUESDAY morning dawned bright and clear, the sky a brilliant soft blue, with a few small white clouds here and there. Laurel had got up early to go for a walk in the crisp, cool morning air before the hordes of mosquitoes and other insects that were a constant menace in the Arctic summer months rose up from the vegetation of the tundra to bite and otherwise torment any human being who had ventured out with areas of exposed skin.

Wearing a warm jacket against the nip in the air, and boots in which she could wade through the patches of boggy ground, she emerged from the medical station, pausing first to draw in several deep breaths of the unsullied air, before setting off at a brisk pace to skirt the village. In the distance she could hear the ice-breaking ships in the Gulf clearing away the huge chunks of floating ice that still clogged the waterway, making a channel for shipping.

There was to be a clinic later on that morning, an adult medical outpatient clinic, that would draw all and sundry who needed medical attention. It would no doubt prove to he hectic, particularly as Bonnie Mae would be preparing Mr Allett for his departure by air—the medevac, as it was called up there. Laurel conceded that she was looking forward to the day, now that experience during the previous month had taught her what to expect.

As she walked her thoughts were jumbled. There was a new professional life to think of. In a few weeks she would be going on to her new job, which had recently been confirmed. Jarrad had not said where he would be going; no doubt it would be to something pretty high-powered. They would have no reason ever to see each other again.

Laurel had been right in her anticipation that the clinic would be hectic.

'The waiting-room's full, Dr Lucas,' Skip informed the two doctors at ten o'clock as they stood together in the outpatient area. 'Can you call in the patients yourselves? I'm going to be a bit busy just now, getting out the charts and X-rays of all these people. Bonnie Mae's organising Mr Allett to go.'

'Sure, Skip! We're quite capable of fending for ourselves,' Jarrad agreed amiably. 'Both Dr Harte and I would just like to give Mr Allett one final check before they go. OK? I did have a good look at him early this morning. . .just want to make sure that nothing has changed. Shall we go, Dr Harte?'

He gave Laurel a sardonic sideways glance, as though daring her to make any reference in front of Skip, however subtle, to the fact that there had been a lapse between them from a strict professional relationship.

'Yes, I'm quite ready, Dr Lucas,' she said stiffly. 'Lead on.' If only he knew how good she was at hiding her feelings, she thought wryly, he wouldn't bother.

'Are you quite with me, Dr Harte?' Jarrad drawled unexpectedly, waiting for her. 'You look decidedly absent.'

'Just thinking about Max, actually. I'm still with you.' Laurel pushed past him, jolted emotionally at the frisson that she felt as her lab coat brushed his.

After Max, she didn't entirely trust such frissons, yet the power to disturb in Jarrad Lucas was undeniable. Keeping her mind focused on him as a doctor, rather than as a man, was considerably more difficult today. The old antagonism had kept her protected against him.

'Morning, you guys!' Bonnie Mae greeted them as they entered the ward area. 'We're as ready to leave as we'll ever be.' The nurse was tall and very fat; her bulk dominated everyone and everything around her. One could tell by her body language that she was very much in charge. 'Mr Allett's great! Just great! Isn't that right, Mr Allett?'

'Compared with my condition the other day, I'm in heaven,' Mr Allett agreed, smiling at them enthusiastically, if a little wanly, from the chair in which he was sitting. 'Now I can't wait to get down south and see a bit of real sunshine—even if I have to look at it from a hospital bed for a while.'

Jarrad took a stethoscope from the pocket of his lab coat. 'Let's take a final look at you before you take off, Mr Allett,' he said, smiling. 'I sure envy you that sunshine.'

Laurel had a small office to herself, where she did initial consultations, then anyone she wanted to examine would be transferred to a cubicle with an examination couch in it, as well as other basic equipment. Here she became ensconced after Mr Allett and Bonnie Mae had departed.

'Here you are, Dr Harte.' Skip came into the office later carrying a manila folder, his round, open face smiling under its thatch of rich black hair. He wore a pristine white uniform suit. 'A new patient for you— a young woman from down south, thirty-four years old. Dr Lucas has already looked at her...he wants your opinion. She's in Dr Lucas's cubicle. I can't pinpoint anything for you on this one.'

The nurses always made a brief preliminary assessment on each new patient, taking a few notes on the patient's complaint, the basic signs and symptoms, then recording the temperature, the blood pressure, the pulse rate, the body weight and the results of a basic urine test, which would sometimes give valuable information about an underlying medical condition such as diabetes or kidney disease. This would speed things up all round.

Laurel found herself hard-pressed not to voice a retort that she was surprised Dr Lucas would ask for her opinion. Instead, she looked through the folder, finding that Jarrad had not left the notes there that he must have taken on the case. 'So this is to be a detective case, is it?' She contented herself with making that innocuous comment to Skip. 'I see that Dr Lucas is keeping his findings to himself.'

'Looks like it.' Skip grinned, 'You can do the same to him some time. We sure get plenty of obscure cases up here.'

With that remark Skip expressed his confidence in her, and she smiled at him. 'OK, Skip, I'll just get on with it.' Seated at the desk, Laurel looked at the basic information about the patient that was in the folder. In addition, Skip had written 'complaining of excessive fatigue, not feeling well'.

Jarrad was standing behind the desk when she entered his equally small office, going over a chart. The look he gave her was unconsciously assessing. 'Hi,' he said. 'I thought you'd like to take a look at this lady...Mrs Landers. Interesting case, I think.'

He put a hand briefly on her shoulder, propelling her in the direction of the examination cubicle, seeming more relaxed with her than he really was, she could tell. Her training had done a lot to help her pick up nuances, as had his; Laurel found herself speculating on whether her feminine intuition gave her an edge over him in that department. Something told her today that she was certainly going to need an edge.

'You haven't given me much to go on,' she said pointedly.

'I thought you'd like to start from scratch.' He looked amused. 'Free from any undue influence. She expressed an interest in seeing a woman doctor as well. Apparently, most of the males she's seen treat her as though she were a psychiatric case.'

'Did you? And is she?'

'No, to both questions. Come.'

Mrs Landers was a tall, thin woman who did indeed look pale and tired as she lay on the examining table in the cubicle off Jarrad's office. The two doctors went in together, with Jarrad keeping in the background while Laurel introduced herself.

'I'm afraid you're going to have to repeat yourself, Mrs Landers, because Dr Lucas wants a second opinion uninfluenced by his own.' The reassuring smile that Laurel gave the tense woman helped to ease the frown of anxiety that creased her forehead.

'I don't mind that. I'm real glad there's a woman doctor here for me to talk to. The men tend to think I'm crazy...at least, the one I saw in Edmonton last year did...had me admitted to the psychiatric floor in the hospital. For assessment, he said. Never did find out what was wrong with me. Not to my satisfaction, anyway. Don't take that personally, Dr Lucas—' the woman looked sideways at Laurel's colleague '—you've been great!'

Jarrad gave her a warm, forgiving smile, and shook his head to indicate that he understood.

'Tell me what your symptoms are. The nurse has written down here that you feel excessively tired,' Laurel said gently, trying to tune out Jarrad's presence close to her. 'I'd like to take some notes.'

'Well...I feel exhausted all the time—which I don't think just has to do with the fact that I've got two active kids, or that living up here can be more tiring than down south in some ways...or that so many things are more of an effort.' Josi Landers spoke thoughtfully, trying to find the right words.

'Do you live up here permanently?'

'No, thank God! My husband's up here for a few weeks to conduct some training sessions at the bank. We're from Edmonton. I can't wait to get back. Anyway, like I said, I'm tired, and a lot of the time I just don't feel right...don't feel well, you know. It's not something I can really put my finger on, I just know that I'm not right.'

'I see,' Laurel said, writing busily.

'I've lost my appetite, I'm losing weight. When I cook for my husband and kids I find that I don't want to eat myself...don't feel hungry. Sometimes I feel as though I'm going to throw up, but I don't...you know, nausea. Also, I have a bit of a fever from time to time, feel myself sweating, then when I take my temperature it's up.'

While Laurel questioned the woman about her background, her medical history and present condition she wrote detailed notes, some possibilities for a diagnosis forming in her mind.

'I've got pain too,' the woman went on, 'in my joints and sometimes in my muscles. The thing is, they're not always in the same joints—the pain seems to move about...I guess that was why the other doctor thought I was crazy. But that's the way it is. I can't pretend it's all in the same place, can I? Just so that someone won't think I'm crazy?'

'No, you can't, Mrs Landers. It's always good to remember, when you feel frustrated in that way, that just because a doctor cannot make a diagnosis on your complaint, it doesn't mean that you haven't got a disease,' Laurel said, feeling a certain indignation on Mrs Landers' behalf. 'Very often the fault lies with the doctor, that he hasn't the knowledge or expertise to make a diagnosis. Like the bad old days, when everything was attributed to witchcraft.'

'Yeah, you're telling me! Call me Josi, Dr Harte.'

'All right, Josi. On the other hand, sometimes it's not possible to make a diagnosis, given the level of our knowledge. We have to admit that we're limited. In your case, I'll do my utmost to get to the bottom of this. You have a rash on your face. How long have you had that?'

'At least two weeks this time. I've had that before, and all. My hair's falling out as well. My hands are puffy a lot of the time—I had to take off my rings. And I get blurred vision some of the time. I thought maybe I needed glasses, but then other times I can see perfectly OK.' Josi Landers nervously twisted her hands as she frequently darted quick glances at Laurel then looked away again, or over at Jarrad.

Laurel felt a rush of sympathy for her. Like many women who were not used to complaining about their own health or life, who had perhaps had their own judgement and illnesses dismissed as nothing, Josi Landers seemed to have at least a partial expectation of being sent away unsatisfied.

'Are you on any medications? The contraceptive Pill?'

'Yes, I take the Pill. Nothing else.'

'OK.' Laurel wrote more. 'I want to listen to your heart and lungs with the stethoscope. You can show me where you get the pains. Then I want to take some blood from you for various lab tests, which will have to be sent down to Edmonton. Unless you've done that already, Dr Lucas?'

'Er—no, I haven't yet...Dr Harte,' Jarrad said, straightening up from where he had been leaning casually against the wall, watching her. 'Please carry on.' There was a certain light in his eyes, something like admiration.

'I'll want some urine from you as well to send down,' Laurel said, sounding efficient and businesslike. 'You could be anaemic too...we can do a blood test for that right here in the clinic.'

'Let me know when you've finished, Dr Harte,' Jarrad interjected, with a formal politeness for their patient's sake. 'I'll be in the office with another patient. I've done all that I want to do.'

It took some time for Laurel to examine Josi Landers very carefully, to take blood for numerous tests, which would go down to the city on the next commercial flight—probably the one that Bonnie Mae was going on. She didn't want to miss anything.

When all those things had been done, Josi Landers looked at Laurel with some trepidation. 'You don't think I'm crazy, then?' she asked tentatively.

'Oh, no!' Laurel assured her. 'I'm not absolutely sure what you've got yet, but one thing I am sure of...it's not all in your mind.'

'Thank God for that.' The woman was close to tears, and she turned her head aside, blinking her eyelids rapidly.

'There's a group of diseases called autoimmune disorders. They're not easy to diagnose, and not always easy to differentiate one from another,' Laurel explained. 'The results of the blood tests will help, and the urine test.

'Rheumatoid arthritis comes into this group, so does multiple sclerosis. I think you may have something known as lupus...maybe systemic lupus erythematosus. The causes are unknown as yet. It's thought to have a genetic component...which may be triggered by something in the environment, sometimes by drugs—even the contraceptive Pill.'

'Is there a cure?'

'Certain drugs are being tried, more in the experimental stage, with some success. What I want to do with you, Josi,' Laurel explained carefully, touching the woman's arm reassuringly, 'is treat your symptoms as they occur—to make life easier for you. This disease produces anxiety and depression, so I can give you anti-depressant medication if you want it. *Not* because I think you're crazy. It will just help you to cope.'

'That's a relief!'

'When I get the results of the blood tests, I'll have a better idea of how to proceed from here. It would probably be a good idea for you and your family to return to Edmonton early, even if your husband can't go. I would like you to have an electroencephalogram there, to look at your brain and nervous system. I know a good internist there who specialises in autoimmune diseases. You need to have an expert looking after you—someone who isn't going to put you into a psychiatric hospital.'

'Yes, that would be what I'd like. That's what Dr Lucas said.'

'Come to see me and Dr Lucas again this time next week...sooner if you need to.' Laurel put her stethoscope back in her pocket and got her notes together. 'I'll give you some medication now to control the symptoms, if Dr Lucas agrees with my diagnosis—and I think he will. I'll want to know what effect they're having on you.'

'OK, Doctor. And thank you!'

'Also, I want you to take your temperature frequently throughout the day and keep a record of it for me, and if you wake up with night-sweats, take your temperature then too. This is going to be like doing detective work until we can make a definite diagnosis. If you want me to talk to your husband about the need to go home early, then I'll be very happy to do so.'

'I feel as though a great weight has been lifted off me. . .just putting a name to what I've got. . .even if there's no definite cure. It could be worse.' Josi Landers smiled up at her.

Laurel continued to talk to her for a while, to reassure her as she labelled the little tubes of blood that she had taken.

'Well, Dr Harte, what's the verdict?' Jarrad was in the cubicle again, peering over her shoulder at the notes she had taken.

'Possibly lupus,' she said.

'That's what I thought.'

After Josi Landers had gone home, they sat down to discuss her. Systemic lupus erythematosus was an intermittent, progressive disease. Patients could live for years with it, although it could sometimes be debilitating.

'Well, Dr Harte, let me congratulate you on your diagnosis,' Jarrad said, his hands wrapped round a mug of coffee as he sat beside her at his desk.

'Are you being facetious? Let me congratulate *you*,' she countered, not waiting for an answer. 'Perhaps we should save the congratulations until we get the results of the blood tests. We could both be wrong, you know. We're neither of us exactly experts on lupus. I can think of several people we could have called upon— and would have—for an expert opinion if we'd been at Gresham.'

'Instead, we have to rely on each other.' He looked her full in the face, and she could tell that he was thinking of how they had lost control the other day.

'That's a new experience. Let's hope we can maintain the trend.'

Laurel sipped her coffee, declining to comment on that. With her emotional antennae at their most sensitive, it seemed to her that there was a definite *double entendre* in his words. Her lips trembled as she attempted to sip her coffee with nonchalance, as she tried to cultivate her dislike; the mechanism seemed not to be working very well. Old longings had been reawakened with his touch, longings and intimations of joy that she had thought were dead.

Josi's condition made Laurel feel depressed. 'If she has got it, maybe she'll be one of the lucky ones—if she takes care of herself, has a good doctor in the city. It's sad to see a young woman with small cnildren to take care of with a chronic disease,' she said pensively. 'It's shameful that she was admitted to psychiatric wards.'

'That's not uncommon. We'll make sure it doesn't happen again,' he said.

'Yes, we will,' she said emphatically.

'Tell me, Laurel. . .what was Max Freer like to work with?' he asked quietly.

'Well. . .' she said, taken aback, 'we. . .only actually worked together when we were students.'

'Not much at all, then?' he said, looking at her keenly with eyes that were cool and shrewd now, eyes that seemed to see such a lot. 'You weren't together much, were you? On duty or off?'

'No. . .' Amazing but true.

'Incredible,' he murmured.

'You know, I'm really enjoying this sort of work,' she blurted out, anxious to get the conversation back on track. 'I had forgotten how enjoyable it could be, a good medical case. Makes a great change after doing surgery exclusively for a while.'

'Sure it does,' he said, fixing her again with his characteristic shrewd, enigmatic regard. 'But then surgery is a man's job, after all. I'm surprised you haven't found that out yet.'

'What do you mean by that?'

'Surgery is a hell of a life for anyone—impossible hours, little or no private life, a hell of a lot of stress, being on call virtually twenty-four hours a day, every day. Even when you go on vacation you're likely to have someone phoning you from afar, seeking you out for an opinion.'

'Why are you doing it, then?' she asked, feeling annoyance rising within her.

'I plan to go into partnership eventually, so that I can reduce the hours I work. Anyway, since I'm a man, someone else is going to have my babies when I'm ready for them. Not so for you.'

'You want babies?' Laurel articulated each word slowly, with an edge of sarcasm. 'I would never have suspected it, Dr Lucas. You amaze me.'

'Some women act as though there's nothing to it,' he said, as if she had not interrupted. 'As if you can just have children between doing everything else. . . then dump them off with strangers to be raised, not really caring what the children want and certainly not asking them for an opinion when they are capable of giving one. I don't subscribe to that view.'

'As it happens, I don't either,' she said, taken aback by the vehemence with which he expressed himself.

'Don't you want children?' he asked her directly. 'Don't you want a normal life?'

'Yes. . .eventually. There's plenty of time. Unfortunately our society doesn't cater to children and their mothers very much, except in a rather rigid way. I. . . don't particularly want the sort of life you've just described. But I don't delude myself that the system is going to change voluntarily for me.'

'Don't turn into one of those hard bitches, Laurel. I've seen too many of them, worked with them.'

'I've been under the impression that you thought I was one of them already,' she said, keeping her voice even with effort. 'And what would you call the male equivalent? I've worked with many of those!'

'I'd call them jerks. Yes, I agree, there are plenty of them. I think there's still hope for you.'

Laurel gasped. 'How very magnanimous of you to say so—' she began heatedly, then gave up in exasperation, determined not to argue with him. 'We *were* talking about lupus. . .'

Skip interrupted, coming into the room to hand Jarrad a folder for his next patient, so Laurel confined herself to flashing Jarrad a look of challenge, compressing her lips into a hard line. He responded with a slight smile, his eyes searching her face. She wondered if he was thinking of how he had kissed her as though he'd wanted to devour her, take her into himself; as though he, like her, had not enjoyed lovemaking and affection for a very long time.

She was glad when Skip began to chat about the patients they still had waiting to be seen. Deliberately she drank her coffee, and then left Jarrad's office silently.

The rest of that morning, and into the afternoon, she saw many patients, with a variety of interesting medical conditions. At two o'clock there was only one chart left on the table in the clinic passage, indicating one more patient left to be seen. After that she could break for a belated lunch, then there would be more in the afternoon.

Looking at the chart, she saw that this was a man in his late twenties, also a new patient, also someone from down south, who was in Chalmers Bay temporarily to work. Apart from Josi Landers and one mine worker, she had so far seen all local Inuit patients, with mostly minor conditions and infections. Skip had written that this man had a large lump at the side of his neck.

With the promise of something to look at that could prove to be very interesting, Laurel went to the waiting-room. 'Rick Sommers,' she called from the doorway.

Rick Sommers looked younger than his twenty-nine years, a good-looking young man with humorous brown eyes and dark, curly hair. 'That's me,' he said.

As he got up from a chair and walked over to her Laurel could very clearly see an irregular large lump at the left side of his neck, starting just above the collarbone, visible through the open buttons of his shirt. The name Hodgkin's disease came to her immediately, as though someone had spoken it aloud for her.

'Come into my office,' she said. 'How long have you had this lump?'

She hoped it would be something else, for his sake, yet the size and shape of the lump, like a classic photograph in a medical textbook, suggested Hodgkin's before anything else that might produce a similar lump. Tuberculosis could produce a growth of the lymph glands in the neck, but generally not like that.

'Well. . .I noticed a small lump months ago. . . didn't do anything about it,' the young man said casually, when he was seated in her office. 'Then just recently it started to grow faster. Can't remember exactly when it started to grow like that. A few weeks, I guess, just before I knew I was coming up here.'

'Have you been to a doctor about it?'

'No. Didn't go to no doctor,' he said cheerfully. 'I figured it might go down.'

As Laurel gently palpated the lump in his neck, her fingers going over it, feeling and probing, Rick lost some of his jocular mood and allowed his underlying anxiety to show through.

'Does that hurt. . .or is it tender?' she said. The lump felt firm, yet freely movable, slightly nodular.

'Nope,' he said.

A phrase from her well-used *Textbook of Internal Medicine*, like many familiar phrases learned by heart over the years, came to her mind—'a potentially fatal outcome'. At least here the lump was visible, an overgrowth of the lymph glands in the neck; sometimes they were hidden in the chest or abdominal cavities, undetectable until symptoms of obstruction appeared.

It was odd that she should see two diseases of the immune system in one day. Not a great deal was known about the causes of either of them, although Hodgkin's disease had been first described a long time ago. It would also be necessary to rule out AIDS.

'Have you had any fevers or weight loss?' she asked gently, trying to put him at his ease, empathising with his attempt at bravado. Although Rick was actually older than she was herself, Laurel found herself feeling protective, like an older sister, apart from in her professional capacity.

'Well. . .yeah, I have, as a matter of fact. . .both,' Rick Sommers said.

'I want to take some blood for tests, Mr Sommers,' she informed him, 'as well as examine you now and take a chest X-ray. Could you come in tomorrow to have a biopsy of this lump? We'd like to take a piece of it to have a look at under a microscope and send down to the labs in the city.'

She knew that Hodgkin's disease produced a particular type of nucleus in the cells of the affected tissue, which should help to clinch the diagnosis.

'Yeah. . .yeah, I reckon I could,' he said.

'You could come in as a day-surgery patient, have a local anaesthetic. Now. . .I would like to get my colleague, Dr Lucas, to have a look at you as well.'

Considerably later, when the clinic was over, it seemed to Laurel that she had been resting on her bed in the annexe for only five minutes when the telephone in her bedroom rang, its irritating buzz jerking her eyes open. Rolling over on her side to pick up the receiver, she saw from the bedside clock that she had in fact been there for almost an hour. It was early evening now, the end of a tiring, if interesting working day. Now the emergency calls would start to come in. With Bonnie Mae gone, Laurel found herself praying that it would be nothing serious.

'Hello,' she said.

'Dr Harte.' Skip's voice recalled her abruptly to duty. It was her turn to be on call that evening, and for the rest of the night. In practice, of course, most emergencies proved to be a double effort—or a triple effort. 'There's a woman here with vag. bleeding. She just walked in without any warning. As far as I can tell from her history, it's an incomplete abortion, very early in pregnancy. At least, she said she thought she was pregnant. . .missed two periods, then started to bleed yesterday, and it came on quite heavy this evening. She thinks she's lost the pregnancy. It's happened before.'

'How's her blood pressure?'

'It's OK for now. I've taken it several times. I've got her on a monitor.'

'OK, Skip,' she said wearily. 'You've done a great job, by the sound of it. I'll be over there in a few minutes. Is there a sterile examination tray? And please get the operating-room ready for a D&C. You know all that anyway, don't you, Skip?'

'Yeah,' he agreed. 'It's the old routine. . .one of them.'

The young woman, whose name was Lori Tuk, was in tears when Laurel saw her in an examination cubicle. 'This is the fourth pregnancy she's lost,' Skip informed Laurel quietly. 'She's twenty-two years old, married three years.'

'Hello.' Laurel greeted the young Inuit woman, then made a quick perusal of her medical chart. It was clear that she had been trying to have a baby for some time but had not been able to do so; each pregnancy had ended in a spontaneous abortion.

'Have you ever been down to the city?' Laurel enquired. 'To see someone at the infertility clinic? You don't seem to have any problem becoming pregnant, but there may be a genetic problem producing an abnormal baby each time, which is one of the reasons why spontaneous abortions occur. Also, there could be what we call an incompetent cervix. . .which I may be able to assess when I examine you.'

Laurel did not believe in talking down to patients. At the moment she had no idea of the young woman's level of intelligence or education, or her knowledge of her own obstetrical difficulties, so for the moment she would assume that she had a good knowledge.

'No. . .I haven't been anywhere,' the young woman conceded, wiping her eyes. 'Maybe now I will go. I'm getting fed up with this.'

'Do you want a baby? And your husband?'

'Oh, yes. Very much.'

Half an hour later they did the dilatation of the cervix and curettage of the uterus to remove the remains of the pregnancy, which would otherwise have become infected and probably caused a generalised septicaemia.

'The cervix is already quite dilated,' Laurel commented to Jarrad, who was giving the general anaesthetic. 'I wouldn't be surprised if she does have an incompetent cervix.' That was the probable cause of the inability of the uterus to hold a pregnancy for more than a few weeks, Laurel speculated, although with all spontaneous abortions the cervix became dilated somewhat anyway.

'Mmm...you're probably right, Dr Harte,' Jarrad agreed, formal in front of Skip.

In light of the remarks that he had made to her that afternoon, Laurel found herself feeling stiff and formal with him—especially now, when the plight of their young patient and her obvious deep grief at the loss of her pregnancy confronted her, Laurel, with the question of her own unfulfilled reproductive capacity.

As she and Jarrad stood beside the stretcher in the recovery room after the operation, waiting for Lori Tuk to recover from the anaesthetic, she realised that she herself had thought about having her own children as a possibility for a rather distant future. It was something that she had taken for granted, yet looking at the face of their patient she felt a stab of an unfamiliar angst.

'She's little more than a kid,' Jarrad murmured, looking down at the smooth, immature face of Lori Tuk. 'And already several failed pregnancies behind her. She obviously married awfully young.'

Laurel darted him a quick glance, with the feeling that he had tuned in to her thoughts. 'Yes,' she said, 'that's the way they do things up here. Motherhood... and making sure that the family survives...is their main function.'

Skip, who had been clearing up the mess they had

made in the operating-room, poked his head round the door. 'I've called in Nuna, the nursing aide, to look after Mrs Tuk during the night. Is that OK with you, Dr Harte? Dr Lucas? She's very competent.'

'Yes. . .thank you, Skip. She can always call me if there's any problem,' Laurel answered.

'That's fine, Skip,' Jarrad agreed. 'I'll stay here for a while, if you want to get some sleep, Laurel—at least until Nuna gets here.' He recorded the patient's vital signs that were displayed on the monitors to which she was attached, his eyes on the computerised screens. 'I want to make sure she's fully recovered from the anaesthetic anyway, before someone else takes over.'

'Thanks,' she said stiffly. 'I'll just hang around until she's fully awake too. I want to make sure that she isn't going to bleed unduly. . .although I'm pretty sure I got everything out.'

'Yeah, I think you did too.' He turned his attention to her. 'You're good at turning your hand to anything and everything, aren't you? I'm impressed. . .more so as each day goes by. And I don't mean to be patronising, even though I may sound like it.'

'That must be difficult for you to admit,' she said lightly, biting back the sarcastic words that she had wanted to utter. 'Are you actually saying that I would be a great loss to the world of surgery?'

'Yeah, I guess I am,' he drawled thoughtfully, after a moment of hesitation. 'But would be even more of a loss to the world of womanhood. I think I can speak with some authority on that. . .now.'

'You can have both worlds in full, can't you?' she shot back, trying not to flush with awareness of his meaning. 'Society allows you that, because you're a man.'

'I don't agree with that entirely. . . As I said before, if you're not careful the job can take over your whole existence, with not much time for a private life. Joshua Kapinsky is a case in point. Perhaps he didn't want a private life...except maybe now, when he's too old to be a father.'

'Leave him out of it,' she said bitingly, her voice low.

'Nature doesn't allow me to have babies. That's a very fundamental dependency that men have on women,' he said quietly.

'And you'd like to make me feel guilty because I have that privilege and I'm not using it? Well...that capacity has its despair and suffering as well as its joys, as you must be aware. Our patient here is an example.'

'Yeah...I know.'

'Perhaps you envy me.'

'Yes...perhaps I do,' Jarrad conceded. His hand, close to hers on the side of the stretcher, moved to cover hers. The recovery room was very quiet. 'You're quite a psychoanalyst, Dr Harte,' he said softly. 'Perhaps you'd like to start on my childhood sometime.'

She couldn't tell whether he was joking. His warm touch seemed to be ringing alarm signals in her body. She wanted her hand to remain beneath his, yet she withdrew it slowly. 'Let me see...' she said. 'Your mother was a hard, bitchy woman who never gave you any attention. So you've been looking for the eternal earth-mother ever since.'

He laughed. 'Pretty good! We'll have to rename you Harte-Freud. Actually, she wasn't hard or bitchy... but the bit about not giving me much attention is true. Even at that time I vowed never to do that to my own kid.'

'I see,' she said. 'Eureka! All is becoming clear.'

'Is it?' He smiled at her cynically, moving his hand over hers again lightly, then removing it. 'I don't think I'm looking for the eternal earth-mother with you, Laurel.'

Just then their patient stirred and began to gag on the plastic airway that was in her mouth, so that Jarrad turned away from Laurel to remove it.

'I'll just check to see how much blood loss there is, then I'll go,' Laurel said. 'If you're sure you don't mind staying for a while.'

'Quite sure.'

It was heaven to get under a hot shower in her own bathroom. As Laurel shampooed her hair, still thinking about babies, she remembered that Max had not been particularly interested in children. Not that either of them had had time to concentrate on anything other then their fledgling careers, but when she had tried to discuss it with him he had simply said, 'Maybe...', in an uninterested way. Busy herself with everything else, she had not persisted.

The sadness was with her again as she got out of the shower, as it usually was when she thought of Max. If only...if only... What a pointless phrase that was! Yet it came back persistently. How easy it would be for her to marry Joshua Kapinsky, a father-figure and husband rolled into one, to wallow in the security that his income would afford. Too easy, perhaps.

When Jarrad came in later she was sitting at the dining-table, dressed in her robe, going over the case histories of the patients that she had seen in the clinic.

'Still up!' He raised his eyebrows at her, shrugging out of his jacket. 'I thought you would have hit the sack long ago.' He strode into the kitchen and she heard him plug in the kettle, then heard the chink of glass on glass as he poured himself whisky and soda, which he did occasionally. Usually he followed that with a cup of coffee.

'Drink, Laurel? Let me mix you something.'

'Um... well, OK. I'll have soda with a dash of whisky, please.'

'Living dangerously, huh?' he teased.

'Mmm. I was hoping you would take a look at some of these notes I made—particularly the ones on Josi Landers.'

'Sure, I'll take a look.' He brought their drinks to the table and sat opposite her. 'So, we're going to biopsy that guy with the possible Hodgkin's tomorrow? Rick Sommers.'

'Yes.' She took a gulp of her drink. 'Since they both come from elsewhere, maybe the best thing for both of them would be to go back home, once we've made definite diagnoses.'

'Yes, I agree. I know someone good in Edmonton who would take on both of them. There is a certain amount of urgency, I think. There isn't going to be any on-going treatment available here, that's for sure.'

While he went slowly over the notes she had made on Josi Landers Laurel watched him surreptitiously, her eyes going over his thick, tousled hair, over the incipient growth of dark beard on his face. There were shadows under his eyes and his skin was pale, like her own.

A desire to reach out and touch his hair reminded her forcefully of how much their relationship was changing, perhaps because of the loneliness of Chalmers Bay. Forcing her mind away from him, she went to the internal telephone extension and dialled the ward area of the medical station. 'Hi, Nuna,' she said. 'Everything OK with Mrs Tuk?'

'Yes, everything's fine,' Nuna informed her reassuringly. 'The blood pressure is one fifteen over sixty-five. Not much blood loss. Less than usual, I would say. She sleeping now.'

'Good. Thanks, Nuna. I'll be going to bed soon,

but you call me if you're worried about anything at all. OK?'

'Sure. OK. Goodnight.'

'Do you want coffee, Jarrad?' she called.

'Yes. Thanks. You sure make thorough notes. That's a good habit to have,' he commented.

He stretched tiredly as she handed him the coffee. 'Thanks.' He swivelled in his chair to look at her. 'Tell me more about Max,' he said.

'Why? What are your motives in asking me about him? You're very persistent. . .like a dog with a bone.' Laurel smiled slightly at the analogy.

'Since we have to work together for a considerable time, I think it would help our working relationship if you were to unburden yourself. You obviously haven't done so up to now.'

'Well. . .I . . . it's difficult to know where to start,' Laurel said, keeping her eyes averted. It was not easy to explain that the physical attraction between her and Max, their need of each other, as well as their mutual fascination with their careers, had carried them over the initial rough time; it was not something that she wanted to say to Jarrad Lucas.

'Try,' he urged gently. 'You've been running away from it, haven't you? There's nowhere to run to here.'

'You're right that I do need to talk about it,' she admitted tentatively, her voice barely audible, 'but I'm not sure you're the right person, Jarrad. No offence intended.'

'Try me,' he offered.

'Well. . .when it was my turn to do an internship, our relationship began to deteriorate. It was almost imperceptible at first. . . Max became irritated with me. . .then really bad-tempered when I wasn't available to be with him on many occasions when he was free.' She glanced at him quickly. 'Do you really want to hear all this?'

'Sure,' he said.

'He forgot how patient I'd been with him when he had done his internship. It was... really awful at times. I guess I retreated into work. I didn't want to face up to the thing with the two of us.'

'I can imagine it,' was all Jarrad said.

'By the end of my internship year,' she continued, on a roll now, not looking at Jarrad, 'the situation between us was strained to say the least. Neither of us wanted to be the one to initiate a break, to even voice the suggestion. The possibility of it just... hung between us all the time, like a tangible weight that was about to fall. We did finally live apart, more by default than by an actual plan. That's about it. We weren't actually living together when he... had the fatal accident.'

'Mmm...'

'What about you?' Laurel met his probing regard defensively. 'You want to know all about me, but you don't give much away yourself.'

'There was someone once. I wanted to marry her,' Jarrad said slowly.

'A doctor?' she said shrewdly. 'A career woman?'

Jarrad laughed in a way that transformed his handsome face, as though not displeased with her perspicacity. 'How *did* you guess?'

'Wasn't too difficult,' she said, smiling back. 'You *are* somewhat uptight.'

'Is that what you call it?' He grinned. 'You're pretty uptight yourself... on the defensive.'

The external telephone in the sitting-room rang then, and Jarrad reached over to answer it. Several times since they had been in Chalmers Bay he had received long-distance calls from women, whom Laurel had assumed to be girlfriends of one sort or another. He had not enlightened her, and had certainly seemed to enjoy talking to them. Laurel found herself becoming tense.

'It's for you,' he said. 'None other than Joshua Kapinsky.' His look was sardonic as he handed over the telephone to her on its long extension cord. 'Don't look so surprised. We're not on another planet here, even though it feels like it sometimes. Have fun!'

As Laurel reached for the proffered telephone she experienced a sharp regret that the rare intimacy she and Jarrad had been beginning to build up by her confidences had been shattered in an instant by this intrusion from her previous life. As she began, hesitantly, to talk to Joshua, Jarrad stacked her patients' charts in a neat pile on the table and left the room.

While it was always good to get a telephone call from 'outside' when one was in an isolated place, and she appreciated that, she found that she did not want a call from Joshua. That was odd, really, when she had recently been thinking about how simple her life could be if she were to marry him.

CHAPTER FOUR

'Pass me the long, blunt scissors, please, Skip.' Laurel pressed a gauze sponge to the operation site, where blood was oozing out over her sterile rubber gloves, and put out her other hand for the scissors.

Suitably gowned, with her head covered by a cotton cap, a surgical mask over her nose and mouth, and plastic goggles over her eyes, she was operating on Rick Sommers the next morning to remove a large piece of tissue from his neck for biopsy.

'Thank you for helping, Jarrad.' She looked across the operating-table at her colleague. 'I expect I could have managed myself, but I just didn't want to risk getting into trouble with excess bleeding. . .nicking the carotid artery, or something.'

'Very easy to do,' he agreed. There was a light of amusement and something else that she could not quite read in his eyes—a protective gentleness, perhaps. 'Anyway, it's my pleasure. . .and this is going to prove to be an interesting case.'

Laurel concentrated on the job in hand. 'I need a large piece,' she explained to Skip, perhaps unnecessarily, 'so that we can send a substantial part of it down to the city in a jar of formalin to be looked at by a pathologist at the university hospital. Another piece I want put in a jar of culture-medium to be sent down to be cultured for possible tuberculosis, to at least rule that out.'

'Maybe we should put a stat order on the specimens for the lab,' Jarrad said as he applied a sponge to the blood that was flowing freely from the wound. 'Then maybe they would get the results back pronto. We could get them to telephone us as soon as they know, then we can at least finalise arrangements to have Rick transferred to Edmonton.'

There was a certain urgency to it all. They both knew that if Rick had Hodgkin's disease he would have to start with radiotherapy as soon as possible. The X-ray that Skip had done indicated that their patient's chest was clear so far, which was a hopeful sign, and the few days of recovery and waiting would give Rick a chance to wind up his affairs in Chalmers Bay.

Using the fine scissors, Laurel carefully snipped the tissue, clamping the small bleeding blood vessels with artery forceps as she went, then with Jarrad's help she tied them off with catgut or used the cautery to coagulate the ends of the vessels by burning.

'You're not going to remove the whole lump, Dr Harte?' Skip queried.

'No. I'll leave that to the surgeons in the city when we transfer him there, if they think it necessary. He's got to go down there for further treatment anyway. I don't want to risk getting into any deep structures, any big vessels that might cause a bleed I wouldn't want to have to control. At the moment I just want enough to make a diagnosis.'

'She's a coward, Skip,' Jarrad teased, with no malice. The remark made Laurel even more aware of how far they had come towards a good working relationship in the short time that they had been in Chalmers Bay; they were beginning to accept each other, warts and all.

'I don't think so.' Skip grinned.

'He's going to need a CT scan, then radiotherapy if he has got Hodgkin's,' Laurel explained to Skip. 'The radiotherapy will shrink the remainder of this tumour anyway.'

Laurel spoke very quietly. Even though Rick had

been given a narcotic drug in his intravenous line to sedate him, as well as having a local anaesthetic at the operation site, he was not unconscious. A person's sense of hearing was the last to go when he was under the influence of an anaesthetic agent or narcotic, and was the first to come back as it was wearing off, so it was always very necessary to be careful what one said in the operating-room.

'If it is Hodgkin's,' Laurel went on, whispering, 'the biopsy will tell me the stage of the disease as well.'

Green sterile drapes covered Rick from head to toe. His head was turned sideways, facing away from them, while they worked on his neck. Only part of his face was uncovered, so that he could breathe and they could observe his colour. Fluid from an IV bag ran into a vein in an outstretched arm, and monitors recorded his vital signs automatically. He breathed slowly and deeply.

Laurel looked at his peaceful, boyish face with a sober feeling of pity, and she felt an almost physical urge to reach forward and cuddle him in her arms, to hold him protectively against her breast like a mother. Just a few years older than she was herself, while looking only about seventeen, Rick was too young to have to deal with what lay ahead for him with this serious disease.

'It's tragic, isn't it?' Jarrad said softly, his head close to hers. Startled, as they communed with each other silently for a few intense seconds, she knew that he was in total intuitive accord with her. A warmth spread through her, a warmth that brought a swift yearning in its wake. . .

'Yes. . .' she whispered. There was little doubt in her mind about the diagnosis.

When the operation was finished and Rick Sommers had been wheeled by Skip to the recovery room, Laurel made haste with the piece of tissue she had removed to the small lab area where there were specimen jars and the necessary preserving and culture fluids to put them in.

Joe Fletcher, their cook, would drive the specimens, packed in a special insulated box, to the airstrip so that they could be on the next plane out. Laurel had already asked him to do it the day before; that was just one of the extra jobs that he did for them. There was one flight that day to Edmonton, which they could not afford to miss.

'Joe's already in the waiting-room, ready for us to hand over the box to him.' Jarrad came to join her in the lab, his face mask dangling round his neck. 'And he's got the pick-up truck out at the front entrance, ready to go. Let me fill out that requisition form for the TB culture.' He came to stand beside her, dominating the tiny lab area.

'OK. The specimen's already in the culture fluid, and labelled,' she said, shifting to make room for him. These days she seemed to be hypersensitive to his physical proximity—more than ever. It was not strictly necessary for him to help her with this.

'We're sure missing Bonnie Mae,' she said chattily, to fill a silence that was loaded with a renewed tension of awareness. 'I guess she won't be back until at least late tomorrow evening.'

'That's right,' he agreed.

Because Bonnie was away, most of the elective surgical cases had been cancelled; they did not have enough staff to look after them in the post-operative period. Nuna had agreed to stay for the morning to be with Lori Tuk, even though she had been up all night.

'I'm anticipating that we can discharge Lori Tuk early this afternoon,' he said. 'That should ease things somewhat. We can take turns visiting her at home over the next week or so—make sure she's OK.'

Laurel had considered that Lori Tuk was her patient, yet she chose to say nothing to Jarrad that would indicate any proprietary feelings. After all, he had given the anaesthetic and they had worked as a team. She told herself that she was being hypersensitive about being taken over.

Rick was awake and reasonably alert when Laurel went to the recovery room a little later to see him, having handed the specimens to Joe.

So far she had not mentioned Hodgkin's disease to Rick, and did not intend to do so until he was fully awake. While he was still under the influence of drugs she would not even hint at a diagnosis. They would keep him overnight, since he had no family in Chalmers Bay to take care of him, and later in the day she would break the news to him, would suggest the next move regarding treatment.

'We'll do those three other minor surgical cases, Skip.' Jarrad accosted Skip outside the recovery room, where they had left a very tired Nuna to keep an eye on Rick Sommers.

'OK, Dr Lucas,' Skip said cheerfully.

'Then I want to examine Lori Tuk,' Laurel chipped in.

'OK,' Skip said again. 'We'll get through it all somehow, until Bonnie Mae gets back.'

And get through it they did. It was a great relief to Laurel to let herself into the annexe at five o'clock that evening, to meet Joe Fletcher coming out.

'Just left your supper there, Dr Harte. I guarantee you'll like that one! Barbecued Arctic char with spicy Cajun sauce, savoury rice, sautéed green beans—originally frozen, of course—with chocolate supreme surprise to follow. I thought of doing Baked Alaska, but figured you might not appreciate that.'

'I can't wait, Joe. It sounds fantastic. Thanks a lot,' she called after him as he disappeared, grinning, along the covered way.

Inside the annexe, she headed for her shower, stripping off her clothes and dropping them on the floor of her room on the way to the bathroom. At the moment she felt as though she had come through a clothes wringer—absolutely drained.

She had explained to Rick Sommers about Hodgkin's disease, giving him some idea of what his chances were, trying to be realistic without being negative. It had not been easy. He had agreed that he should be transferred to Edmonton as soon as she could set it up for him, which should be within a week, to coincide with the arrival of the diagnosis. By having done the biopsy in Chalmers Bay she hoped to have saved precious time for him. The sooner the radiotherapy was started, the better.

In addition to that, she had examined and discharged Lori Tuk, whose mother had come to the medical station to take her home. It was up to the young woman now whether she wanted Laurel to make arrangements for her to go to the city to see a consultant obstetrician.

The shower in Jarrad's bathroom was running when she came out to get her supper, now ravenously hungry. Obviously he would be joining her to eat, and she found that she was not averse to the idea. It felt good to be dressed in jeans and a casual loose sweatshirt. Joe had left most of their food in the oven, apart from the chocolate supreme surprise, which was sitting in a very prominent position on the kitchen counter in a glass dish.

She got out cutlery, plates and glasses, deciding to open a bottle of white wine from their very limited, very precious stock of wine. There was nowhere to buy wine in Chalmers Bay, it had to be ordered from down south and picked up from the airstrip. That didn't deter some people from drinking a lot, as she well knew, although they generally preferred hard liquor, which caused quite a serious health problem in the community.

'At last, a pause for a decent meal, eh, Dr Harte?' Jarrad said somewhat sardonically when he came in the room and took in the preparations she had made. He loomed big in the small space, looking somehow more aggressively masculine in jeans and an open-necked checked shirt. 'I don't really expect you to do the "little woman" act, you know.' He paused to watch her as she put the finishing touches to the table.

'You could have fooled me! I shall expect you to take your turn tomorrow,' she said tartly. They sat down to eat, helping themselves from the dishes.

'What did old Josh have to say?' Jarrad queried unabashedly, after they had been eating for a while. 'Is he still proposing marriage? Still got the hots for you? Which I assume he did have, of course...'

If Laurel had not felt mellowed by half a glass of wine she might have let rip at him with her sarcasm. As it was, she contented herself with a prim pursing of the lips. 'If you must know, I haven't slept with him—as I think I said before when you so politely hinted that I had. I assume he's a full-blooded male.'

'Better not make that assumption.' There was teasing amusement in his glance as he willed her to look at him. As though on cue, she blushed. 'Have some more wine, Laurel.' He lifted the bottle and refilled her glass, the smile widening his sensual mouth.

'You're really adorable, you know, when you've got a bit of wine inside you. Pity I didn't know that when we were at Gresham. Funny expression, isn't it... sleeping with someone? When what we don't do is sleep. I don't suppose you've missed much with Josh.'

'Will you shut up?' She did not want to admit that she understood him, that he was able to move her.

'Are you going to marry him, Laurel?'

'I'm very tempted. Now, will you sh—?'

'No. . .' He cut her off. 'He would be good as your daddy, but not your kids' daddy.'

'Why should you care?'

'I don't. Idle curiosity, that's all. It would be a waste too, of course.'

She stood up, exasperated, trying not to let him see how much his words affected her. 'Let me get you some chocolate supreme surprise, courtesy of Joe Fletcher,' she offered with exaggerated sweetness. 'Then you can serve me tomorrow.'

'Sure,' he said. 'Thanks.' He leaned back in his chair indolently. 'How about a trip to the local tavern after supper? There's a song contest there. . .should be fun to watch. I've already asked Skip to check up on Rick Sommers and Nuna from time to time—to call us if necessary.'

'What if I don't want to go to a song contest?' Laurel said loudly from the kitchen, noisily getting out coffee-cups.

They had been to the Golden Nugget tavern before, once or twice. It was a run-down drinking place that periodically had noisy goings-on that went under the name of 'entertainment'. The entertainment aspect of it was generally inadvertent, Laurel thought ruefully, yet she did need to get out somewhere before a sense of claustrophobia settled upon her.

'Come anyway,' he called back. 'When you're married to old Josh you may never again get to see such original entertainment. It will be the ballet, classical concerts, chamber music. . .but not the kind of chamber you like, Laurel.'

'Will you stop calling him "old Josh"? It's rude and demeaning, which he doesn't deserve,' she said with exasperation, plonking coffee-cups and dessert dishes on the table. 'I can picture the sort of woman you'll marry...your earth-mother!

'She'll have hairy legs, big floppy breasts with no bra to hold them up, no make-up, of course, and hair tied behind with an elastic band... *au naturel* in everything—including sweat. She'll work in a health-food store, bagging lentils...part-time, of course. She'll have a baby every year, until you have at least ten, and she'll think that the sun rises and sets on you... that goes without saying.'

Pausing in her diatribe, standing with hands on hips, she watched him laugh, realising that this was the first time she had ever seen him really laugh unreservedly. The sight did something to her—something that left her feeling incredibly susceptible to him again, while resenting even more what he had said about Josh as she made the inevitable comparison between them.

The corners of his eyes crinkled up in a very attractive way and she found herself staring; she could see his even white teeth and she remembered what it was like to be kissed by him. Then she reminded herself that she didn't really like him; it wasn't difficult, when all she had to do was recall the unpleasant scene that had taken place in the cateteria at Gresham hospital. Accordingly, she hardened her heart.

'I don't particularly like lentils, or women who bag them,' he said at last, still smiling. 'As for marriage...I don't intend to marry for at least five years. I manage to get plenty of female company without it for the time being.'

'You mean sex,' she said.

'That's what women always understand men want,

isn't it?' he said. 'I won't bother to deny that, since I don't suppose you'll believe me.' He stood up to face her. 'When I want my babies, I'll look around.'

'For a brood mare,' she muttered.

'Mmm...' he agreed, smiling. 'Tell me...why did you marry Max Freer? He was a bright guy, but not, I think, quite up to you. If you weren't quite such an obvious—what shall I say?—career woman...you would be quite something. You're just a little too calculating, Laurel. Or is it all defensiveness?'

'And who asked you?' she exploded with equal rudeness, hurt yet again. Their light-hearted teasing was taking a strange tack, with unfathomable undercurrents. 'That's what I call a back-handed compliment. Perhaps you're scared to pay me an outright compliment in case I presume too much! Well, don't kid yourself!'

'I wouldn't do that with you, Laurel,' he said softly.

'You aren't exactly all spontaneity yourself,' she went on, something goading her not to give it a rest. 'You're something of a cold fish. I've always thought so. Self-contained, not letting anyone really close to you, as though there's a glass wall around you. So what happened in *your* past to make you so uptight? Tell me that!'

He came to her then, taking up the space between them in two steps, while she just stood there.

'I loved Max when I married him,' she said, her emotions taking a vulnerable turn. 'How can you say I'm calculating when you don't know? You never forget or forgive, do you? You don't give an inch. Yes, I was young and stupid...but I loved him.' Horrified, she heard her own voice wobbling with emotion, felt her lips trembling.

'Oh, hell...' he said under his breath. 'I seem to have done it again.'

'Can you honestly say you've ever loved someone?' she demanded.

'Yes...yes, I can,' he said quietly.

While she fought for composure, feeling that there was something else behind his apparent teasing, he spooned out dessert into the small glass dishes. 'Here,' he said, 'open wide.' Taking a spoonful of the chocolate mixture, he offered it to her. Obediently she opened her mouth while he fed her, knowing that he was trying to apologise.

'Mmm...delicious,' she conceded when he had finished spooning the contents into her mouth.

He had successfully deflected another emotional show-down. Once again, they had gone so far and no further. It was as though they had come to the brink of something, had both been frightened to take the step over an invisible but very definite line. Laurel fought down an urge to bawl her eyes out. It had been a hard day.

The Golden Nugget was filled with raucous noise when they entered it later. Dimly lit, decorated with gilt and mirrors of a poor quality, it looked like the rundown set of a second-rate movie about the old Wild West. Yet there was a certain charm about it, uncontrived.

They were lucky to find an empty table for two. Laurel subsided gratefully onto a rickety wooden chair while Jarrad fought his way through the crowd near the bar to buy drinks for them. A band of sorts was tuning up on a small stage; one man had a mouth organ, another a fiddle, another a piano accordion. The singing competition was getting under way.

When they had been there for about five minutes, a huge man dressed in blue jeans and a red and black checked shirt, with a large paunch hanging over his substantial leather belt, got up to sing. He was unshaven and obviously merry from the effects of the drink he was holding. He grinned out at the expectant audience, showing several gaps in his front teeth.

'I left my heart in Kansas City. . .' he yelled tunelessly, then paused, obviously having trouble remembering the next line—if indeed there was one.

'If that's singing,' Jarrad commented sardonically in the pregnant pause, leaning close to Laurel, 'then I'm Luciano Pavarotti.'

Suddenly Laurel began to giggle uncontrollably, tears running down her face, shoulders shaking. She leaned on the table and put a hand over the lower half of her face.

'Don't let that guy see you laughing at him,' Jarrad suggested lightly, smiling, raising his eyebrows at her loss of control, 'he could be offended. I couldn't guarantee to defend you if he got belligerent. He's a little bigger than I am.'

'I think you could out-fox him,' she spluttered, hardly able to control her features. 'I'm going to enjoy this.'

About two hours later they walked back to the medical station in the twilight that was almost as bright as day. Laurel, for one, was feeling considerably more cheerful. They had left lights on in the annexe, and the squat building looked as welcoming as it ever would do as they approached.

'I want to go over to see Rick Sommers before I go to bed,' Laurel said when they arrived back at the medical station.

'I'd like to come with you,' said Jarrad, making a detour to the exterior door of the clinic. 'When are we shipping him out?'

'As soon as it can be arranged. Within a week, I hope. Now that he's had this little operation,' Laurel reflected, 'he'll have had time to ruminate on his condition, so maybe he's having trouble sleeping. I did prescribe something for post-op pain.'

'Yeah. He might be ready for a bit of tender loving care,' Jarrad murmured as they entered the clinic.

Nuna, who was sitting in the ward area where Rick had been transferred, got up when she entered. 'Hi, Dr Lucas... Hi, Dr Harte,' she said. 'He's a little restless.'

'Hello, Rick, how are you feeling?' Laurel sat down beside the bed where Rick was propped up against several pillows, the thick dressing on his neck distorting his shape.

'It's pretty painful. It comes in spasms. I'm having trouble sleeping.' Rick held himself stiffly, so that he did not have to move his neck, rolling his eyes to look at her. 'I'm worried too—wondering how I got this thing.'

'Can you swallow and breathe normally?' Jarrad asked, inspecting the dressing.

'Yeah... My neck feels pretty stiff, though, as well as the pain.'

'We'll give you an injection to take away the pain. It will also help you sleep,' Jarrad said, giving Rick's hand a reassuring squeeze. 'Did some of your friends come in to see you this evening?'

'Yeah... I've got some good friends up here. I called my family in Edmonton too, like I said I would, so they know I'm gonna be coming home soon. I just have to call them again as soon as I know the flight.'

'We'll book the flight for you when we've finalised the arrangements with the hospital there. Try not to worry too much about it right now, Rick. Just concentrate on getting over this operation,' Jarrad said as Laurel got up to prepare an injection for him.

'I'm going to give him fifty milligrams of Demerol,

which should be enough to tide him over for a while so that he can go off to sleep,' Laurel said to Nuna. 'Watch for undue swelling of the neck, as I said before, and make sure he can breathe and swallow. I see you've got the emergency intubation tray handy. Good.'

As she talked to Nuna she could hear Jarrad talking quietly, reassuringly to Rick, and she was glad that he was there with her. In a few moments she had given the intramuscular injection.

'Call one of us immediately if there's the slightest hint that he's having trouble breathing. Watch him carefully, and keep him in that semi-sitting position,' Jarrad instructed Nuna again, when they were out of earshot of Rick and as he looked at the chart.

'I see the blood pressure's OK. Keep taking that. . . we want to be sure there's no bleeding at the operation site. We may have to keep him here another day, or longer. We'll see how he is tomorrow. He might be better off here.'

'OK, Dr Lucas.'

In her own room later, Laurel washed her face and hands and brushed her teeth. A soft knock came on her door just as she was tying the belt of her robe over her nightdress, and the sound caused her heart to jump with an oddly fearful excitement. Her fingers were clumsy as she fumbled with the lock that secured her door.

As soon as she opened the door she knew instinctively that Jarrad was offering her a chance to invite him into her room, into her bed; it was not necessary for him to say anything, or even to change his expression very much. The subtle invitation, the desire was there in his eyes, in the stance of his body as they looked at each other. There was a certain point beyond which he would not go, would not presume, until she had made her move, she could sense that.

'I didn't say goodnight to you,' he said softly. 'And I wanted you to know I enjoyed your company at the Golden Nugget...very much.' The dressing-gown that he wore covered only his nakedness, she suspected, even though her eyes did not stray from his face.

'Oh...well, I enjoyed it too. It was a...a great suggestion.' She mouthed the words automatically, feeling that a transition was slowly taking place in her under his intense scrutiny—a change from doctor to private woman, someone with desires and needs of her own...desperate needs. This was the first time he had really addressed her as a woman, on what seemed like neutral ground between them.

'I'm glad you think so,' he said. A mesmerising silence lengthened between them as they stood very close.

Oh, God, don't let me weaken. Don't let me make a fool of myself, Laurel found herself thinking as her eyes moved to his partially exposed chest and she felt as though she were choking with her desire to sway forward against his strong body, to feel his arms tighten round her again. If only he wasn't so damned attractive, exuding that indefinable masculine sex appeal by merely existing. Perhaps then she would have had a better chance to resist him.

'What an awful thing to have happened to Rick— he's so young,' she blurted out. 'I...I feel so desperately sorry for him. It's so depressing.'

'There are worse things,' he said. Then, as she held herself tense, her heart thudding, he touched her. With the back of his hand he traced a line delicately down her cheek and along the line of her jaw. The touch brought comfort—she knew he intended that—nonetheless, there was an unmistakable sexual element. Her intake of breath was sharply audible in the absolute quiet of the annexe.

'You're an innocent, really, aren't you, Laurel Harte?' There was a certain wonder in his tone. 'I'm just beginning to realise. Who would have thought it?'

As he spoke he moved his hand slowly to the back of her neck, under her swath of hair, his fingers cool on her skin. Shivers of an exquisite anticipation seemed to feather her body like a caress.

'Does that surprise you?' she whispered, not able to hide the automatic defensiveness that she felt with him.

'So you don't deny it?' he said huskily.

'No. . .' Her need of him was escalating to a point where she knew that soon, if he did not withdraw, she would be touching him in return, would be loosening the belt of his robe with frantic fingers so that she could feel his hardness against her soft, yielding femininity. . .

Reminding herself of her basic dislike of him, she tried to recall the humiliation and rancour of that cafeteria scene in Gresham to bolster her contradictory emotions. But as she tried to focus on it, it became in her mind like a cameo scene in an out-of-date play. It was no longer real. The real was the here and now—his face, his mouth, so close to her own, his hand delicately caressing her sensitised skin.

They both moved simultaneously then, so that their mouths came together in savage, hungry contact. Her muffled cry of assent, deep in her throat, was echoed by his sensual, long drawn-out murmur of pleasure as her arms convulsively circled his neck and she moved the few inches that brought her tight up against him, firmly into his embrace.

Time lost all significance as they stood locked together as one body, one mind. In moments Jarrad's robe had come open, and Laurel found herself delirious with joy when she could actually run her hands over the naked, warm skin of his broad back, his shoulders, could move her hands down to the taut muscles below his waist. All at once it felt so right, so very right.

Long moments passed as their mouths clung, as he threaded his fingers through her hair to hold her face close to his. She did not object when he slipped her robe from her shoulders, when it rustled to the floor around her feet; neither did she object when his hands covered her breasts warmly, then moved smoothly over the indentation of her waist.

Without thought for anything else other than the feel of him, of the exquisite sensations he was evoking in her, she matched him in the intensity of his need, move by move, as he murmured incoherent words of encouragement to her.

'Oh, Jarrad... Jarrad...' Laurel spoke his name as though it were new to her, her voice soft and tentative, yet tense with a longing that he could not fail to recognise.

Jarrad's hands were smoothing over the delicate silk of her long nightdress. 'Take this off, Laurel.' He spoke the words huskily, his cheek against hers.

Laurel's hands stilled and she held her breath, a sensation of something like horror coming over her, an awful feeling of *déjà vu*. Mundane, common as those words might seem out of a particular context, they now held a significance for her that was most likely out of all proportion to Jarrad's intent.

Max had said those words to her so often in similar circumstances. In her mind she could hear the exact intonation of his voice.

The last time Max had wanted to make love to her she had not wanted him; it had been at a time when she'd suspected that he already had a girlfriend, when things had been going downhill between them. He had merely wanted to use her, Laurel, like an object.

'No...no!' Laurel drew back abruptly from Jarrad, thrusting him away from her wildly, almost expecting to see Max there, smiling in that knowing way of his. 'No, I can't...I'm sorry.'

'Laurel, what's wrong? Tell me!' Jarrad's voice seemed to come from a long way off as she backed away from him, up against the door of her room that had swung shut behind her.

'I just can't,' she said, her eyes staring at Jarrad, her fingers fumbling for the doorknob behind her. 'I'm sorry...I'm sorry.' At last her fingers found the handle and she turned it.

The door yielded behind her. Turning from Jarrad, a need to cry tightening her throat painfully, she entered the sanctuary of her room and slammed the door.

Tears blurred her vision then. Max had betrayed her innocent, girlish trust; perhaps he had destroyed her chances with other men for ever. What had made her think, for those few glorious moments when reason had deserted her, that she could trust Jarrad Lucas any more than she had been able to trust Max? More than she could trust any man?

CHAPTER FIVE

'IT's really great to have you back, Bonnie Mae,' Laurel said, with feeling, as the two of them were having a very belated coffee-break at one o'clock in the afternoon on Friday. 'To say we missed you is an understatement.'

Laurel sat with her shoes off, her aching feet propped up on a chair as she sipped her coffee. Joe Fletcher had brought them a large plate of sandwiches.

'I thought you might,' Bonnie Mae said, her plump face dimpling as she smiled. 'One thing I ain't, and that's modest!' She wore one of her custom-made uniform trouser suits that helped to disguise her very ample figure. This one was a pale pink. 'I'm glad we've finished operating for the day already. I've got a few things I have to catch up on here.'

'Yes, so have I. If you don't need the pick-up truck, I want to do a few home visits. There's the girl who had the incomplete abortion to see, and I want to take Rick Sommers home, see what sort of set-up he's got there. . .He spent the last two nights here because we didn't feel happy about letting him go.'

'Sure, you take the truck. I don't need it.'

'How long have you been in Chalmers Bay, Bonnie?' Laurel asked curiously. 'Interesting though it is, I don't think I could take it for more than a summer myself. The very thought of the winter makes me shudder.'

'Well. . . I've been here six years. The Northern Medical Development Corporation is real good to me. If I want a break, they just get someone else to take

92

over for a while. This may actually be my last year up here full-time. Chuck—that's my boyfriend—and I are finally getting married in October, down in Edmonton. We've sure waited long enough, I can tell you!'

They were still chatting when Jarrad and Skip came in to help themselves to coffee and sandwiches. 'Is this woman-talk?' Jarrad queried, acknowledging Laurel's presence with a quick, intense glance. She felt herself returning it—a secret exchange, out of her control. 'Or can anyone join in?'

'It's people-talk,' Bonnie Mae said. 'I'm just recounting a few anecdotes from my professional past.'

For another fifteen minutes they ate, drank and listened to Bonnie Mae until she reluctantly stood up. 'Well. . .I've got a lot of catching up to do, folks. I guess you want to phone down to the city to find out how Mr Allett is, Dr Harte? He was OK when I left him.'

'Yes, I plan to do that this afternoon.'

When Bonnie and Skip had gone out, Jarrad put down the newspaper he had been pretending to read, and as Laurel looked up at him from where she was sitting the tension escalated to an unbearable degree. For moments neither one spoke. Laurel had managed to avoid him at breakfast time.

'This is what you might call an atmosphere that one could cut with a knife. . .wouldn't you say?' Jarrad commented with a fake lightness.

'I'm sorry. . .' was all that she could think of to say as feelings of humiliation and regret competed with other emotions dredged up from the past—things that she had thought yesterday were buried for ever.

'Don't be sorry,' he said as he leaned against the sink behind him, his arms folded across his chest. 'It's not your fault. If anyone should be sorry, it should be me. But I don't think "sorry" really comes into it. I'm sure not sorry I kissed you. Are you?'

Laurel looked at the floor, studying the pattern on the worn carpet. 'No,' she said truthfully. 'No, I'm not.' If she had said otherwise, he would have known that she was lying anyway.

'You want to talk about it? Later, maybe? This is not the place.'

'No. . .no,' she said hastily, 'I don't think so. Not yet, anyway.' Who knew what that might lead to? And she wasn't ready. She felt churned up inside, as though she were about to sit for an exam for which she was ill-prepared.

'Let me know when you do,' he said brusquely now, standing up straight, so close to her and yet so far away. 'And for God's sake, stop feeling sorry. That might be some sort of start for you.'

With that parting shot he was striding from the room, leaving her sitting alone to experience a feeling of having been deserted. Max Freer always seemed to stand between her and Jarrad, as did, to a lesser extent, Joshua Kapinsky.

How she wished now that she could have handled the situation differently last night, instead of acting like a colt startled at the sight of a branding-iron. At least that image made her smile wanly as she got up to return to work.

The pick-up truck that belonged to the medical station was an unwieldy beast, Laurel decided, not for the first time, as she drove it slowly along the wide, unpaved track that served as the main street in Chalmers Bay, carefully steering around the larger pot-holes that were filled with water from melted snow.

Rick Sommers was at her side on the passenger seat, his overnight bag on his lap. They were going back to his temporary home in the village, where he had lived with friends while he was working there.

His flight home to the city was booked for the following Tuesday. They had received telephone verification that the diagnosis was Hodgkin's disease; they were now waiting for the written report. Bonnie Mae had changed Rick's neck dressing that morning and Laurel had inspected the wound to make sure that it was healing as it should.

'Well—' Rick broke the silence '—I'm not sure how I feel about leaving this place. Wonder if I'll ever be back.'

They chatted about life in Chalmers Bay until they arrived at the small one-storey house that Rick shared with two young friends who worked for the same oil exploration company in the dock area which employed him—one of whom had stayed home to be with him that day. To Laurel the house appeared comfortable— a place where she felt happy to leave Rick in the care of his friends.

'Would you come up to the clinic on Sunday, Rick, so that I can look at your dressing again? I'd like to take out the remainder of the skin clips. Get in touch if there's anything worrying you before then, and I'll finalise the arrangements with the hospital down there for your admission next week.' They shook hands as she was leaving. 'Take care,' she said.

'Thanks a lot, Dr Harte. See you Sunday.' For a few seconds Rick Sommers allowed the vulnerability that he was feeling to show in his eyes, then he smiled as she left.

There was really no way that she could soften the blow of the diagnosis, Laurel conceded as she walked back to the truck in a sober mood that was matched by the utilitarian surroundings. All she could really do was give him hope because his disease was in the early stages and could be treated. The sooner he got down to a major hospital, the better.

Lori Tuk was next on the agenda. Lori and her young husband lived with Lori's mother in an unpretentious prefabricated house. As they sipped tea in the main living area they discussed the possibility of a visit to the city hospital.

'You could stay down there for a week,' Laurel said. 'The Northern Medical Development Corporation has a house down there now, where you can stay free of charge. . .you just have to buy your own food. I could make all the arrangements—your appointments, and so on.'

Lori looked at her shyly. 'I have been thinking about it. . .I would like to go some time, but there's no way we could afford the airfare now—we are a poor family. And I wouldn't want to go alone. . . I've never been out of Chalmers Bay.'

They talked for some time, trying to iron out all the difficulties. In the end, they left it that Lori and her family would consider it carefully. Somehow a cheap flight out would have to be arranged.

Living and working in a place like Chalmers Bay was so different from being in a city, where it was relatively easy to plug into sophisticated services, Laurel reflected as she left them to walk the short distance to where she had parked the truck. The people in Chalmers Bay took very little for granted. All they were really sure of was that the snow would come. She knew that it was not up to her to make decisions for these people; she could only tell them what was available and offer to help.

The next call was on Josi Landers—more of a social call, as the results of the lab tests were not yet back, and to find out whether the drugs that she had given her to control symptoms were working.

Again, Laurel drank strong, sweet tea, mixed with condensed milk from a tin. Josi's thin, tired face became animated as she chatted with Laurel.

'It's good to have a visitor. Not that I'm isolated here. People are coming in and out all the time—mainly my husband's friends, or the kids' friends. I've discussed with my husband about going back to the city. He'd like to come with me, otherwise he'll worry about me, so he's looking into winding up his business here as soon as he can.'

It was later than Laurel had planned when she finally clambered up into the cab of the pick-up truck for the return journey to the medical station. A thin rain began to fall as she carefully skirted the pot-holes and avoided the few other trucks that shared the road with her

As there were no roads out of Chalmers Bay, there was little traffic. In the good weather, people either walked or used three-wheeled all-terrain motorised bikes; then, when the snow covered the ground—which was for the best part of the year—they used skidoos or dog teams.

'Business is booming!' Bonnie Mae called to her in a stentorian voice as soon as she entered the clinic. 'Dr Lucas is scrubbing for an emergency Caesarean section with Skip, and we've just had a call from the RCMP—there's been a crash of a light plane out on the tundra, near one of the mine airstrips.'

'I see what you mean,' Laurel said drily. 'I won't bother to take my coat off, then.'

'They want one of us to go out there to the site with them. There's a Cessna about to take off from the airstrip here, and one of the RCMP guys is on his way here to pick one of us up. You want to go, Laurel?

Apparently there are no really serious injuries—maybe a broken leg or two. You could take the basic emergency kit.'

'Sure, I'll go. I can feel my interest perking up already. Just what I need.' As she spoke she heard a truck come to a halt outside.

'That will be Wayne Keeling,' Bonnie Mae said. 'He sure ain't wasting any time! Here's the emergency box. Better not keep the guy waiting.'

Laurel had met Wayne Keeling and Greg Farley, two of the Royal Canadian Mounted Police officers stationed in Chalmers Bay, soon after she had arrived in the community. They were a very important and stable element there.

'Laurel!' Jarrad's voice brought her to a halt as she reached the door, about to exit with the emergency box in one hand and her general medical bag in the other. 'Now that you're here at last, maybe we should make some other arrangement. You sure as hell took your time out there.'

The old sarcasm, that she had been willing to forget about, was back in his attitude. He held his arms up in front of his chest, dripping water, having come from the scrub sinks. 'Maybe you should do the C-section, and I'll go with the RCMP. I had no idea when you would be back—you didn't tell us.'

There was censure in both his voice and his expression which brought embarrassed colour to Laurel's cheeks before the shrewd scrutiny of Bonnie Mae.

'I don't agree. It would be better if you went ahead with the C-section, since you've examined the patient and know her history, whereas I haven't even seen her,' Laurel responded. 'It would save time. I make it a rule not to operate on someone whose medical history I haven't read, and I guess there is a certain urgency. Wayne Keeling's already here, anyway. Someone has to go right now.'

'I think that's more my job,' Jarrad said coolly. 'A man's job.'

Bonnie Mae and Laurel exchanged looks. 'I do that stuff all the time, Dr Lucas,' Bonnie Mae said. 'Not so long ago, we didn't have any doctors up here—male or female.'

'It's my place to go,' he persisted, his lean face taut. 'I'm concerned for your safety, for God's sake!' Irritation made his voice harsh. Bonnie Mae raised her eyebrows and wisely absented herself from the scene by squeezing past him with a pointed 'Excuse me'.

'In that case, I'm definitely going,' Laurel said, forcing an emphasis into her voice as she felt a cool frisson of alarm displace her earlier sense of accomplishment after the home visits.

Something was goading Jarrad into this confrontation with her; that something, she didn't doubt, had a lot to do with their emotional confrontation of the night before.

'The C-section obviously has to be done right away, and I don't think it's appropriate that I should just walk in here and scrub, when you're already scrubbed and ready to go ahead. I shall be quite able to cope out there. One thing I am not, Jarrad—I'm not a wimp!' She pushed her untidy, windblown hair away from her forehead with rising agitation.

'I'm chief here. Remember?' He was like the old Jarrad, coolly assessing and strictly professional, as he stood before her in his operating-room gear, staring her down, his eyes dark with suppressed anger.

'I was wondering when that would come up,' she muttered, loud enough for him to hear.

They were interrupted then by Wayne Keeling barging in noisily through the door. 'Hi there, Dr Lucas,

Dr Harte! All set to go, Dr Harte?' His jovial, no-nonsense manner cut through the atmosphere in the room as he saw that she was the one wearing the coat and carrying the equipment. 'Let me take that gear.'

With barely a glance at Jarrad, Wayne Keeling took the emergency box from Laurel and was ushering her in front of him and out of the door, a hand on her upper arm, before she could utter another word. Then she was running after his tall, uniformed figure as he strode to the RCMP truck.

A flash of frenetic humour came to her as she followed, with an absurd desire to shout after him, Hang on a minute, Wayne, till I've had an argument with my chief! She could imagine his mouth opening in amazement, his succinct reply.

Within minutes they were rattling back through the village on the road she had just travelled, going towards the airstrip, too late now for any second thoughts on her part.

'We've got a Cessna all ready to take off,' Wayne informed her, not letting her get a word in edgeways. 'Makes things easier when there's an airstrip at the other end, eh? Although we can land on the tundra if we have to. I'm coming with you.'

The thrill of being airborne, of flying relatively close to the ground in the small Cessna and thus being able to get a wonderful view of the tundra, was somewhat spoiled for Laurel as she simmered with feelings of anxiety, anger and regret over her verbal exchange with Jarrad. It was the first time, too, that Bonnie Mae had witnessed any major difference of opinion between them—even though she had tactfully absented herself from the scene early.

It was important for good working relations that they should present a united front. Resentment at Jarrad for having shattered that harmony compounded her annoyance. She hadn't thought that he would actually come on as the heavy. Memories of their passionate kisses vied incongruously with her recent experience.

Patches of snow and ice still dotted the tundra, as well as pools of water in all shapes and sizes. Noise from the engine precluded any conversation as she and Wayne Keeling sat behind the pilot in the single-engine plane. Forcing her thoughts ahead, Laurel planned what she would do when they got to the site. Meanwhile, any distraction on her part would scarcely be noticed, she hoped despairingly.

'There she is...the Carter Lake mine.' Wayne Keeling mouthed the words at her, pointing ahead and over to the left.

When Laurel craned forward to look she could see buildings far below, then a lake beyond them—presumably Carter Lake. As they gradually lost height they could see the mine's airstrip where the crashed plane, looking like a toy from that distance, was askew near it. The two wings appeared to be intact.

They circled the mine twice, losing height, before making a bumpy landing that brought their aircraft down as far away from the crash as possible, then the pilot moved their craft overground to within a few yards of it.

Two men were lying on the ground, with several others hanging around them, as Laurel and Wayne Keeling stepped down. A stiff wind was blowing in from the tundra, bringing with it moist, sweet air. Perhaps it was this wind that had caused the pilot of the downed plane to make an error of judgement.

As she walked towards the crash site a mental picture of how things must have been for Max when he had had his accident flashed suddenly before her mind's eye. That had not happened to her for some time.

He had been alone in the car, had crashed on a cold, wet night. For months after the accident Laurel had not been able to pass any sort of road accident, or see pictures of one on television or in a newspaper without a feeling of dread coming over her, without seeing him lying on the road. Because she had not been there she had felt guilty for that as well.

'Hi there, Wayne!' One of the bystanders greeted them as they approached.

'Hi!' Wayne called. 'How you-all doing?' Wayne, originally from Newfoundland, occasionally lapsed into the vernacular. 'This here's Dr Harte, come to fix up all yous guys.'

Laurel's boots squelched in mud as she stepped off the runway onto rough ground. She was aware that the men were all rapidly sizing her up. The two injured men lay on the ground on plastic sheets covered with blankets, their injuries not immediately apparent.

She shook hands quickly with all those standing. 'What are the injuries?' she asked, carefully placing her bags on part of a plastic sheet.

'Well, there was only one guy in the actual plane—that's Doug,' the mine manager spoke up. 'He overran the runway, as you can see. As near as we can make out, both his ankles are broken and an arm as well—the left arm. The right shoulder seems to be dislocated. Maybe there's a cracked rib or two—that's why we didn't want to move him too much. Otherwise, it's bruises and bumps.'

'I get the picture,' Laurel said, kneeling down beside the men, lifting up a blanket.

'The other one, John, he's one of ours—a miner. He was helping the other guy out of the downed plane,' the manager continued in his calm drawl, 'got his hand slammed in the door...got two of his fingers cut clean off. He's in a lot of pain. So's the other guy. We did what we could for them.'

He spoke with the assurance and calm of someone who had seen it all before, who was used to coping with disasters and accidents of all types.

'Have you got the fingers?' Laurel said, bending down to rummage in her medical bag as the wind whipped around her, pulling at her clothing and hair.

'Yep! We wrapped 'em in a clean cotton neck-tie.'

'That's great. I want to take these men's blood pressure, to see if there's any bleeding to speak of, then I'll give them both a shot of morphine.' She straightened up, holding her stethoscope and sphygmomanometer. 'Then it will be a question of getting Doug splinted in various places, including a neck brace, and getting them both onto the stretchers.'

The men helped her as she needed to free of clothing an arm on each of her patients in order to take the blood pressures. The man with the two severed fingers had a large pad and firm bandage over his hand, through which there was a small amount of blood seeping.

'Well, so far, so good,' Laurel commented after the check. 'There's no bleeding to speak of. The pressure is a little low on both of them, which could be accounted for by shock. While the arms are bare I'll give the morphine.'

It took only a few moments to inject the two men with the painkilling drug. She would wait for it to take effect, then she would splint the injuries. 'Where are the fingers?' she asked the foreman. 'Maybe there's a chance that they could be reattached, if we can get on with it pretty soon.'

Silently the man handed over the small cotton scarf in which the fingers were wrapped. Trying not to look too closely at them, Laurel placed the fingers in a sterile jar of normal saline that she had brought in her bag and moved them around in the liquid to wash any dirt off them, watching the liquid turn pink.

If there was anything she felt squeamish about, it was severed fingers and toes, and mutilated hands in general—even though she took great satisfaction in trying to work with such things in the operating-room. It was all very different in an ordered, sterile setting.

'I'll have to put on a pair of sterile rubber gloves to fish them out,' she explained to the men, who were watching her movements in a respectful and slightly horrified silence. 'They need to go in another jar with a different solution—Ringer's lactate. That's a suitable medium in which to transport them and preserve them for possible reattachment later.'

They continued to watch her as she put the second jar in an insulated box and packed it around with dry ice. The fingers had to be kept cold, but not frozen.

'Ready for the splints, Dr Harte?' Wayne Keeling broke the mesmerised silence, no doubt judging that the two injured men were suitably sedated.

'Yes,' Laurel stood up and turned to the manager. 'Could you get a message through to the medical station for me, please? Tell them exactly what injuries we have here. Tell Bonnie Mae that I'll need the operating microscope—I'm going to have a go at reattaching these fingers, and maybe Dr Lucas could help me. For Doug, we'll probably need some screws to put in the fractured arm and maybe the lower legs. As you said, the right shoulder joint is dislocated too, at the acromio-clavicular joint. OK?'

'Yep.'

'Will there be any problem having five people in the Cessna?' she asked Wayne, not sure of the maximum capacity of the small aircraft.

'Nah,' he said breezily, 'we've done it before.'

Hours later Laurel was still looking through the operating microscope in the glare of the bright lights of the operating-room at the medical station. In the absolute quiet of intense concentration, both she and Jarrad were putting the final touches to the operation that had reattached the fingers, using sutures finer than a human hair on nerves and tiny blood vessels to reconnect them.

They sat opposite each other, knees almost touching, with the large operating microscope between them; it had a separate eye-piece for each of them. The injured hand was under the powerful lenses, resting on a small sterile table. Whether the operation would be successful, whether the two fingers would 'take' after the time-lapse, remained to be seen.

They had dealt with the fractures of the other man, Doug, first. Laurel had arrived back to find everything ready and in the busy time that had followed she had not had time to consider any atmosphere between herself and Jarrad; he had been strictly professional.

They would keep both men at the medical station overnight, then have them flown out, accompanied by Skip, the next morning.

It was the middle of the night when Laurel finally went to her own room and gratefully shut the door. Her exhaustion was compounded by her realisation that all was not right between herself and Jarrad. He had been distant and aloof when they had finished work.

They now had three overnight patients in the medical station, including the woman who had had the Caesarean section earlier. Nuna was there looking after all of them, together with the newborn baby.

Laurel undressed quickly and put on her light bathrobe, resolving to get to sleep as soon as possible and fully expecting to be called out at least once in what was left of the night. When a knock came on her door she was very reluctant to open it, knowing that it would be Jarrad.

'I want to talk to you,' he said. He looked pale, exhausted.

'Can't it wait until tomorrow? I'm desperate for sleep,' she said bravely. This was no time for a show-down.

'So am I.' He came into her room and shut the door. 'No, it can't wait. I want to get this off my chest now.'

When she retreated to the centre of the room he followed her, looking as grim as she had ever seen him.

'I didn't appreciate having you contradict me in front of Bonnie Mae this afternoon, having you question my judgement. You put me in a very difficult position.' His face was taut with anger, his eyes blazing as he regarded her.

'I. . .I consider that you put *me* in a difficult position,' she said, facing him. 'You contradicted *me*. And I stand by what I said then. There was no time to get into a long discussion.'

'If anything like that happens again,' he said, as though she had not spoken, 'I shall be forced to contact the NMDC and have you removed from here—or have myself removed, whichever is the most expedient at the time and depending on how bloody fed up I am with you and this place in general!'

Shocked by his vehemence, Laurel swallowed to dispel a sudden painful constriction in her throat. 'You start a job, you finish it. . .unless there's very good reason why not,' she managed to say. 'I have always understood that. Look, we're both tired. . .'

'I don't appreciate you doing a number on me in

front of the staff,' was his tight-lipped reply.

'I don't understand what you mean...."doing a number",' she denied, wishing fervently that he would go, feeling tears prick her eyes.

'Don't give me that!' he said viciously. 'It's something you're pretty good at!'

'I think you've said enough,' she managed, her lips trembling. 'Getting things off your chest seems to be a habit with you. Why can't we just get along with each other? Why did you have to pull rank, Jarrad? We were doing so well.'

'I was not pulling rank,' he said, articulating each word clearly through gritted teeth. 'I was simply trying to organise the work for maximum efficiency and safety. Yes...safety! Perhaps that's something that had not occurred to you?'

'My safety, you mean? I was thinking of the *patient's* safety—the woman. And how many times have you been out on the tundra in a light plane?'

'That's immaterial.'

'No...no, it isn't.' Tears were obvious in her eyes now as she fought for control. They were both breathing fast, their anger fuelled by their exhaustion. 'If... if this has anything to do with...with what happened between us last night, I think it's inappropriate for you to get at me this way...'

His lips twisted in a smile of wry self-mockery in which there was no humour. 'I'm not desperate...if that's what you're implying,' he said. To her fraught senses, the remark implied insult.

'Get out of my room.' The words came out on a sob. 'Get out!' She took a step closer to him, bringing her arm up to hit him, scarcely aware of what she was doing. Deftly he caught it, holding her tightly, so that she was almost up against him. So different from last night...the bitter thought came to her.

Obviously he was thinking the same thing as his eyes raked her face, his expression one of cynicism. For seconds their eyes held as her tears spilled over onto her cheeks, then she felt she would choke with tension as he looked at her trembling mouth, at the 'V' of bare skin exposed by her robe.

'Glad to,' he said, abruptly letting her go to walk to the door. 'This is strictly business, Laurel.' He paused at the door. 'Don't forget what I've said.'

As soon as he was out she locked the door hastily, then let the tears fall. Last night he had wanted to make love to her. . . He had wanted her for a long time—even when they had been at Gresham. Certain things had become clearer in Chalmers Bay, and she knew that last night *she* had wanted him.

If only she were not so utterly tired, she told herself as she went to her bathroom, a hand over her mouth to stifle the sobs, she would be far better able to cope with Jarrad Lucas. What a mess it all was—what an awful mess.

CHAPTER SIX

JOHN, whose severed fingers had been sewn back on, departed from Chalmers Bay on a very early flight the next morning to Edmonton. A friend had elected to go with him, and Skip drove them to the airport.

The fingers looked reasonably good, if a little blue, Laurel considered as both she and Jarrad inspected them prior to John's departure, which would indicate that at least they had succeeded in reconnecting the blood vessels so that he would have an adequate blood supply—enough to prevent gangrene from setting in.

'I'm not so sure about the nerve supply,' Jarrad had said, when John had been unable to move the fingers. 'That's why it's urgent for you to get to a centre where there's a surgeon who specialises in microvascular work, who can operate to connect the severed nerve-endings more adequately than we've been able to do. Otherwise, John, you might have two useless fingers that you can neither move nor feel.'

Fortunately, they knew such a person in the city, had duly written him a letter for John to take with him, and had telephoned the hospital to make sure that the man was not on holiday and to alert them that John was on his way.

As for the other injured patient, Doug Rayner, they had decided to keep him at the medical station for several days, then he too would fly out to his family in the city and to the hospital there. He did indeed have two fractured ribs, which they had taped up and intended to watch closely. There was always the possibility that the fractured ends of the ribs would perforate the lungs if Doug made the wrong movements.

Laurel was used to working under stress, so the disquiet between herself and Jarrad was just something else that she added to her daily ration, without any outward indication.

On the morning that Rick Sommers was due to leave Chalmers Bay, Joe Fletcher arrived at the medical station with their mail bag from the post office, which had come up on a very early flight.

'There are lab reports for us, Dr Harte.' Bonnie Mae greeted Laurel with this information when she put in an appearance at the clinic, having come over extra early to get through some essential work.

'Thanks, Bonnie. I've got Rick Sommers coming up here this morning for a final check before he departs. I hope his lab report is here; I'd like to get that confirmed.'

'It is here. You want me to change his dressing, Dr Harte?'

'Yes, please, Bonnie.'

Being seriously pressed for time and exhausted simultaneously did help to concentrate the mind wonderfully, Laurel thought cynically as she pushed the recollection of Jarrad's recent annoyance to the back of her mind yet again. It had a way of persistently intruding.

She pressed her fingertips against her eyelids, trying to ease the physical ache engendered by lack of sleep, that was combined with an odd mental anguish. Methodically she went through the mail until she found the pathology report that pertained to the biopsy that she had done on Rick Sommers.

'Hi, I thought I heard you getting up at an impossible hour.' Jarrad came into the clinic office as she stood with the reports in her hands, making her jump.

'You're looking somewhat despondent.'

He was obviously determined to be very professional, neutral and polite; only his eyes held a slightly wary, assessing look as he greeted her. It was amazing how quickly things could change between people, Laurel considered, looking up.

'Hi,' she said.

His hair was slicked down with water from the shower, and Laurel could smell the distinctive aftershave lotion that he used—a subtle combination, she decided, of ginger, lime, cloves and other undefinable ingredients. It made a welcome change from the ever-present odours of anaesthetic agents, of iodine and other antiseptics that persistently pervaded the clinic.

'What's the definitive verdict on Rick Sommers?' In a moment he was standing close to her, looking over her shoulder.

'Well. . .' she said, shuffling papers and steeling herself against him, separating out the report on Rick Sommers. 'Let me see. . . In direct, precise language, it's what we suspected and what they said on the phone; he does indeed have Hodgkin's disease.' With a sigh, she handed him the slip of paper.

Even though they had been told the diagnosis verbally, the stark confirmation triggered Laurel's incipient depression, and she felt instinctively that this was not going to be a good day.

'One hopeful thing on the horizon,' Jarrad murmured, still looking at the report. 'It confirms that the disease is still in the early stages, which makes successful treatment a possibility.'

'Yes. . .' she agreed. 'The blood reports on Rick are here too. . . The ESR is up—he's anaemic. Here's something else. . . Josi Landers definitely has lupus too,' she said slowly.

One of the things that Laurel liked about Jarrad was

that he was always professional when he had to be, she considered with a reluctant admiration, watching him look through the reports. He seldom stepped out of line on the job; he was somehow able to switch off his personal life. Judging by his stance now, they might never have been in each other's arms, might never have had a disagreement either. Did she, Laurel wondered, appear as cool to him as he seemed to her? It was the way he had been at Gresham, of course.

'Mmm...' Jarrad handed the reports back, his eyes going perceptively over her pale face. 'You've told Rick, haven't you?'

'Yes... but I'll have to go over it again this morning, before he goes. I'll have to consider exactly what I'm going to say to him, now that treatment is the predominant issue.'

'Radiation is pretty effective in shrinking the tumours, in combination with chemotherapy,' Jarrad said. 'Unfortunately, sterility could be one of the side-effects of that treatment.'

'Does he know that?'

'I haven't brought up the subject yet. He could donate sperm to a sperm-bank prior to the treatment. Do you want me to talk to him about that?' Jarrad offered, very matter-of-fact.

'Yes, if you would... please. It's not that I'm being coy—I don't feel that I can speak authoritatively on the subject.'

'Right! We'll both have a go at him later when he turns up. OK?'

'Yes,' she said.

Rick was a really sweet guy, she thought again later as they faced each other across the limited expanse of the desk in her cramped office. His warm brown eyes regarded her steadily as she confirmed the diagnosis that he had feared, then he listened attentively as she assured him that there was hope of a cure in his case.

She spoke slowly and carefully, choosing each word, to make quite sure there would be no misunderstandings, and without talking down to him. When patients were under stress such as this, it was common that they did not really hear what was being said to them, did not take it in. 'Now,' she said when she had finished the explanation, 'Dr Lucas wants to talk to you about certain side-effects of the treatment.'

'I wonder how I could have got this,' Rick said, yet again, looking down at his clasped hands when she had stopped talking.

'It's nothing you've done. . .so don't blame yourself,' she said gently. 'As I said before, it's possibly caused by a virus. . .'

Laurel let him talk then, and listened while all his anxieties poured out, making no move to go, to hurry him up. Probably in the city, in the frenetic pace of a large hospital, there would be no one with the time to listen to him, really to talk to him with the empathy that he needed.

'Will you keep in touch with me and Dr Lucas, Rick. . .as well as with the clinic in general? I'll want to know what's happening. I'll come to see you when I'm passing through Edmonton at the end of the summer. And of course I'll be in touch with the doctors at the hospital; they'll keep me informed of the treatment.'

'Sure, I'll stay connected,' he assured her, gratified that he was not going to be abandoned by the Chalmers Bay clinic, or by his friends there.

'I'm going to hand you over to Dr Lucas,' she said, standing up. 'Then Bonnie Mae will change the dressing. Keep the wound dry until it's completely healed.'

'OK. Thanks again, Dr Harte.'

A very quick cup of coffee was in order, she decided,

before she located Jarrad and before she continued with consultations in the outpatient clinic. Rick might appreciate some coffee too.

She was not far from tears when she poured herself a cup of the hot liquid in the general office of the clinic after she had carried a cup to Rick, then she allowed the moisture to gather unheeded in her eyes until her surroundings became blurred. When someone came in to join her she kept her head averted, blinking rapidly.

'How did it go?' Jarrad spoke curtly just behind her.

'Oh. . .not too badly. It seems a little odd, shipping our patients out a lot of the time. But I suppose it isn't really much different from the city, where we're referring people all the time and may never see them again.' She glanced at him quickly and saw him register the moisture in her eyes.

'Yeah. At least in the city the referrals are often within the one hospital, so we can keep in touch if we want to.' As Jarrad stood near her she was aware of vibes that she could not instantly interpret. Perhaps he wanted to apologise. Well, she was in no mood to make it easy for him—if indeed that was what he wanted.

'Anyway, he's in my office, waiting for you,' she said.

'Ok, I'll be with him in a couple of minutes. I want you to know that I had a call yesterday from the Black Lake gold mine. They want one of us to go there to do some routine checks on the staff. I thought I would go,' he said smoothly, 'unless you particularly want to make the trip.'

Laurel looked up at him, controlling her features with a supreme effort. 'You go, by all means,' she said. 'When would you go?'

'Maybe next week. I'll wait till Doug Rayner's out

of here. I would be there for one full day, with a half-day at either end, coming and going. I'd stay over the two nights.'

'OK,' she said, feeling that he was testing her in some way. 'I'm not going to put up an argument, Jarrad, if that's what you expect. It's a different situation.'

Bonnie Mae's entry to the office precluded any further discussion on the matter, and Jarrad left.

The clinic continued, busy as usual. There was no need for Laurel to confer with Jarrad on anything else. Morning ran into afternoon, then afternoon into early evening. Work engendered a certain calm in Laurel, so that she was almost regretful when it was over.

Walking back to the annexe through the covered way, she was looking forward to the tea that she was going to make and to the sandwiches that Joe Fletcher would have made for them, with maybe a cake to go with them. In her room she washed her hands and face, then added a little make-up to her pale skin. Without bothering to take off her scrub suit, she went to the kitchen to boil a kettle.

When her mouth was full of smoked salmon sandwich and she had a mug of steaming tea in her hand, someone knocked on the outer door, the one that went directly outside. On the doorstep, when Laurel opened the door, was a young woman in an airline uniform, looking very tanned and very glamorous, smiling a broad, white-toothed smile. Laurel swallowed hastily.

'Hi,' the young woman said; it sounded like 'haa-aah'—a very long drawn-out drawl that was surely not Canadian. 'I'm looking for Dr Lucas. . . Jarrad. I'm a friend of his from way back. Just come in on a flight. Haven't got much time—we take off in an hour or so. Is he around?'

'Um, I could call over to the clinic for him. Come

in.' Laurel stepped back to let her in, admiring as she did so the young woman's immaculate air stewardess's uniform that fitted like a second skin, moulded to her seductive curves, and contrasted very vividly with Laurel's own crumpled scrub suit. The voice was recognisable from some of the telephone calls that Jarrad had received over the weeks that they had been there.

'Thanks a million!' the girl gushed, scarcely looking at Laurel, no doubt gearing up for her meeting with Jarrad. 'Tell him it's Ginny, in for a flying visit. That will sure be a surprise! I don't usually get this run. . .I managed to fix it for once. Well—' she looked around her critically '—what a cubbyhole this is!'

'I'm Dr Harte, by the way. Laurel Harte.'

'Oh, yeah. He mentioned you.' The girl focused momentarily on Laurel with her lovely, somewhat vacant, green eyes that were fringed with long lashes heavy with mascara. Full, pouting lips, that were lipsticked bright red to match her fingernails, made a little moue of dismissal as she looked somewhat disparagingly around the homely sitting-room. 'I thought somehow you'd be older. . .from the way he described you, you know.' She gave a trilling little laugh.

'I'll call Jarrad,' Laurel said. 'If you'd like some tea, help yourself from that pot. OK?'

Bonnie Mae answered the phone. 'Gee, I'll tell him. Maybe that's just what he needs. He's been in a really withdrawn mood all day! You better make yourself scarce, Dr Harte, so that he can get a bit of tender, loving care, eh? We've got a couple of women in labour on their way here, anyway, so I'm going to need you—and maybe Dr Lucas too. Wouldn't you know it? They always seem to come in twos. . .must be the power of suggestion, or something.'

'He'll be here in a moment,' Laurel informed Ginny, then, as she replaced the telephone receiver, she felt a rare chagrin at Bonnie Mae's words, at her assumption that Jarrad needed loving care. To prepare herself for more work she bit into another sandwich in the kitchen, not wishing to witness a reunion between two people who were perhaps old lovers.

'Great!' Ginny gushed from the other room. It sounded like 'graay-aate'.

Ginny ran across Laurel's line of vision through the kitchen doorway when Jarrad finally appeared, then she practically threw herself at him, flinging her arms around his neck as he stood stock-still to take her weight. 'Jaarr-aad. . .you doll! Surprise!'

'Ginny! What the hell are you doing in Chalmers Bay, of all places?' Jarrad's tone held indulgent amusement as his arms went firmly around Ginny's nubile body, while over the top of her immaculate blonde head his eyes met those of Laurel as she stood facing them, chomping on yet another sandwich with determination. It was obvious from the way his handsome face lit up that the surprise was pleasurable to him, and Laurel felt a stab of fierce jealousy.

Swallowing hard, then washing the bread down with a mouthful of tea, she quickly averted her eyes and walked over to the door to the covered way. The sight of the girl in Jarrad's arms was suddenly unbearable. 'We have two babies to deliver very soon,' she announced curtly, telling him what he probably already knew. 'So I'll see you over there in about twenty minutes or so. . .doll!'

Having made what she thought was a good exit, she gave way in the privacy of the bleak passage to emotions that threatened to swamp her. It was very clear to her now that she was jealous, that she had developed feelings of possession for Jarrad Lucas. Maybe she would not be so blasé at their eventual parting, after all.

CHAPTER SEVEN

'WHAT did you think of Ginny?' Jarrad asked Laurel casually later that evening, breaking the silence when they were drinking tea in their sitting-room after a busy few hours delivering babies. There was no way that they could avoid each other.

Jarrad was smiling slightly, as though the recollection of Ginny brought him a certain satisfaction. 'She's the sister of someone I knew once. She works for Whitelands Airways and somehow got herself transferred up here for a few runs.'

'Well, she's. . .er. . .um. . .' Laurel muttered. 'I don't know. Why ask me? I didn't get to talk to her much. She wasn't interested in me, apart from making a comment that she thought I would be older from the way you had described me. I wasn't flattered by her tone.'

'She said that?' He was still smiling, 'Ginny isn't known for her tact. . .or for her brains, for that matter.'

'So I assumed,' she said drily. They were making a determined effort to be civil to each other and Laurel was feeling the strain, wanting nothing more than to go to her room, have a shower and go to bed for a long, uninterrupted sleep—which was becoming a luxury. When she was with her colleague like this, there was a sense of poignant regret that she didn't know how to break. 'She's definitely not your earth-mother,' she added, draining the last of her tea and standing up.

'No, her talents are in other directions. Maybe I told

her what a fantastic surgeon you were, which is why she thought you must be older,' he murmured.

'I'll bet!' she said sarcastically. 'Goodnight.' She wanted to get away from him before the annoyance she was feeling, fuelled by jealousy, showed on her face, which felt stiff from the effort of achieving apparent neutrality.

'Laurel. . .wait a second.' He stood up too. 'About the other evening—'

Laurel interrupted him. 'Don't say any more now, please. Goodnight.'

Josi Landers came up to the medical station later in the week to have her diagnosis confirmed.

'I feel a lot better, actually, Dr Lucas.' She spoke to Jarrad, as Laurel stood by. 'Those tablets you gave me for the depression, Dr Harte, seem to be starting to work. . .leastways, I feel brighter. And the ones you gave me for the night-sweats are helping too.' Josi sat beside Laurel's desk and smiled. Having had a name put to her disease had definitely lightened her mood, regardless of the eventual outcome. 'I can live with knowing what I've got,' she added.

'The rash on your face seems to have toned down somewhat,' Laurel commented. 'You've been using the ointment I gave you?'

'Yes, I sure have. Now I don't mind looking at myself in the mirror so much. I used to avoid it before.'

'You will have periods of remission, when you'll feel reasonably well—something like multiple sclerosis. Have you and your husband decided yet when you'll be going back?' Jarrad broke in gently.

If only he would be as nice to me, Laurel thought wistfully.

Perhaps if I'd let him, he would be. . . A persistent

voice, of her alter-ego, or something, spoke up perversely.

'He's decided to leave it up to me whether I go without him,' Josi said. 'I know he wants me to wait for him...he's trying to wind everything up here as fast as he can. The minute I feel I'm getting worse, I'll go anyway.'

During the following week, on the Wednesday, Doug Rayner was flown out. He would need follow-up treatment with an orthopaedic surgeon, then later he would need physiotherapy, but from X-rays taken before his departure it was clear that the fractures appeared to be healing.

Jarrad had arranged to fly out to the Black Lake mine on Wednesday afternoon, and come back on the Friday. There were only three very minor operations scheduled for that day. They were day-surgery patients that Laurel could deal with herself.

'Call me if there's any problem here,' Jarrad said coolly to Laurel as they ate lunch together in the annexe, prior to his departure. 'I can be back here quite quickly, depending on the type of transportation,' Jarrad added.

In his usual highly efficient manner, he had given her the numbers and details of how to contact him at any time of the day or night; she knew exactly where he was going to be at all times. The mines, like the medical station, had very sophisticated communications equipment, as well as their own planes.

'Yes, I will,' she said lightly, determined to keep everything on a strictly business footing.

Late in the afternoon, when Jarrad had long gone and the operations had been over for some time, Laurel took the pick-up truck to visit Lori Tuk and to call in on the new mothers and their babies at home.

Mothers and babies often went home on the day of the delivery, or the day after.

When the visits were over, Laurel turned the nose of the truck in the direction of the open tundra beyond the airstrip. The main road went on for a short distance and then petered out into a bumpy dirt track, then stopped altogether and gave way to a growth of low scrub—mostly Arctic willow, one of the few things that would grow there among the briefly flowering hardy Arctic blossoms.

There was a blessed silence when she got out, apart from the ever-present muted sound of wind as it moved over the tundra. From far out on Coronation Gulf the siren of a ship sounded briefly. There would still be ice in the water, huge, thick chunks of it that never completely melted.

For over an hour she stayed there, lying down on the flat rock, allowing herself to doze. The beeper that she had in her pocket, on which she could receive a message from Bonnie Mae if she was needed, remained silent.

On the drive back to the medical station she picked up the mail from the post office, gratified to see that there were several letters for her from her family. As usual, she was less sure about the one from Joshua. Back in her room, that letter rang a few alarm bells as she read it; he again asked her to marry him, yet there was a definite tone to the letter that suggested he was thinking rather of *when* they would be married, instead of *if* they would be married. Laurel had an uncomfortable feeling of being pressured.

It felt odd the next day to be without Jarrad, yet in other ways she welcomed the breathing space that his absence offered.

'Laurel, there's a woman here with a five-month-old

baby that looks pretty sick to me,' Bonnie Mae announced to her halfway through the morning, coming into her office where she had been seeing patients for the outpatient clinic.

'What are the symptoms?' Laurel paused in the writing up of notes at her desk.

'The kid has had a cold and cough for three days—with a fever, the mother thinks...didn't actually take the temperature...then he started vomiting in the night and this morning.' Bonnie Mae came in and shut the door. 'I've checked him out and he definitely has a high fever and some signs of cerebral involvement. There's a rash and some bruising too. It don't look good to me...and the parents are pretty young and naïve. I know them, and the baby.'

'Oh, dear.' Laurel got up. 'Hope this isn't the start of some sort of outbreak. Lead me to him.'

'We've had meningitis up here before—several times,' Bonnie Mae said, standing solidly in the doorway, hands on hips. 'That's my guess. It's no fun, believe me!'

'I can imagine!'

'As it was, the last time I thought three of them were goners for sure, but somehow they made it. One of them seems to have minimal brain damage, though, and I suspect it's a consequence of that epidemic,' Bonnie Mae went on.

The young Inuit mother stood by silently while Laurel examined the baby, who alternated between lethargy and irritability, obviously not liking being handled. Movement caused him pain.

Laurel took her time, to be sure of not missing anything that would be vital. As the nurse had said, it did not look good. The rash and bruising, indicating that the clotting mechanism of the blood had gone awry because of an overwhelming infection, suggested meningitis. Once or twice the baby broke into a high-pitched irritable cry, reacting excessively when she touched him, and there were involuntary twitchings of his muscles.

'You've got a paediatric lumbar puncture tray, I assume, Bonnie?' she asked quietly.

'Sure have! It's right here...together with all the other stuff that we're likely to need.'

'Good. Do we have any fresh plasma on hand? I'll want to start him on some of that.'

'Yes, we always have two or three units of it—it comes up from the city with our supply of blood for transfusion,' Bonnie Mae said.

They sent the young mother to sit in the waiting-room after Laurel had explained to her that her baby possibly had meningitis. They did not want her to have to witness the lumbar puncture, which her baby would not like—although he would, of course, be given some local anaesthetic.

They would have to put a needle into his back to get a specimen of the cerebrospinal fluid, which would have to be sent to the lab in the city for culture and sensitivity tests to determine the precise diagnosis— the type of bacteria that were responsible for this particular case of meningitis. Then they would also know the precise drug to which it was most sensitive.

There would not be time, however, to wait for the results of any such tests; they would have to start treatment immediately, or the baby would die.

'That's it, then,' Bonnie Mae said, with an ominous inflexion in her tone, as they both watched the cerebrospinal fluid come out under pressure when they had the needle inserted, whereas it should have dripped out slowly.

'After we've fixed this kid up I'd better get on to the RCMP to let them know that we might have an epidemic on our hands. They usually go from house to house dropping off leaflets...you know, telling people that they should bring children with colds and coughs or with any other symptoms to the clinic. What next, Doc?'

'I want to take some blood for tests, to send to the city, as well as this cerebrospinal fluid. And, Bonnie, after you've spoken to the RCMP, would you mind contacting Dr Lucas at the mine? Tell him what's going on, ask him to come back as soon as he can finish up there.'

'Sure.' Bonnie Mae gave her a shrewd look, but did not comment on why she, Laurel, would not make the call herself.

'No one argues with you, Bonnie,' Laurel commented, deciding to be up-front with the nurse.

Bonnie Mae chuckled. 'You're right-on there, Doc! If they do, they only try it once. I'm the uncrowned queen of Chalmers Bay, all right!'

'Have we got ampicillin and cephalosporin in stock?' Laurel asked, straightening up to ease her aching back from where she had been bending over the child. As always, her mind was well ahead of her actions, thinking of all possibilities, all angles.

'Yep! We sure have! We've got everything in this place except leeches...I see to that! And I bet I could get them if I had to!'

Bonnie Mae was at her best when challenged, Laurel could see that, and she was very grateful. They gave each other a slight, conspiratorial grin, both relieved in their reliance on each other, both happy to pool and share their expertise and experience.

'I'd like to put him on both those drugs, then... give him a couple of shots immediately,' she said thoughtfully. 'Then I want to put up the IV plasma...I may have to do a cut-down to get into a vein. And I want to insert a naso-gastric tube so that we can give him some fluids that way.'

'Right! I've got all the equipment here,' Bonnie Mae said. 'We can get on it right away.'

'I'm going to decide later whether to keep him here or get him on a plane... He's so ill, he might not survive the journey the way he is now. That's why I want Dr Lucas back here—for a second opinion.' It was not necessary for her to spell it out to Bonnie Mae that Jarrad was likely to pull rank on her again if anything went wrong. Besides, she needed him—in more ways than one.

'OK, Doc. I just have to get the plasma from the lab. Poor little fella, eh? He don't look too happy.'

Skip answered the telephone in the afternoon when the call came through from Jarrad to say that he was at the airstrip in Chalmers Bay. 'I'm taking the truck to go get him,' Skip announced to Laurel and Bonnie Mae.

'OK, Skip. Make it snappy,' Bonnie Mae said.

By late that evening two more cases of paediatric meningitis had appeared at the clinic. The RCMP, alerted earlier to the possibility of an epidemic, had distributed information around the community, detailing the signs and symptoms of the infection. All staff members were in the ward area, doing what they could for the sick babies.

'Monitor the intravenous plasma carefully, Bonnie, and make sure the IV antibiotics are given on time.' Jarrad spoke to Bonnie Mae and Skip as they all stood by the bedside of a sick baby. 'And we have to at least make some attempt to keep each baby isolated from the others, in case they're not suffering from exactly the same infection. And watch the urine output...we may have to pass a few catheters—something I'd like to avoid if we can.'

He ran a hand wearily over his untidy hair, then pulled down his face mask as he moved away from the bed and absently stroked the day's growth of beard on his face. Watching him, Laurel was very glad of his presence; it was some time since she had seen a baby with meningitis.

'I've telephoned to the city for more drugs and plasma to come up on the next major flight,' Bonnie Mae said as she took off the rubber gloves and gown that she had been wearing to attend to the baby, but leaving her face mask in place. 'That's early tomorrow.'

'Why don't you take a break, Dr Harte?' Bonnie Mae suggested at eleven p.m. 'There isn't any more you can do here right now. We'll monitor them and give the drugs. One of us might as well get some sleep.'

'OK,' Laurel agreed. Up to then she had been too keyed up to consider her own fatigue. Now she was aware that she had been slowing down for some time.

'Dr Lucas will be back over here soon, after his bit of shut-eye,' Bonnie Mae said. 'In the meantime, I'll call one of you if anything comes up.'

Back in her own room, Laurel whipped off her disposable cap and stroked a brush through her glossy hair until it tumbled around her face, full and soft; it made her feel human again, instead of a sort of automaton that only had to make life-and-death decisions and act upon them, with no room for anything else—least of all room for error.

After two hours of exhausted sleep, that seemed to have passed like five minutes when her alarm clock woke her, she got up and put on a clean scrub suit. Thrusting aside her own tiredness, she walked briskly through the covered way and back to work.

The first person she saw on entering the ward area was Jarrad. Suitably gowned, masked and gloved, he held a small baby up against his chest, the head supported tenderly against his shoulder, his own head inclined slightly towards the infant's, as though giving comfort to the tiny scrap of humanity.

The sight of him in such a stance gave Laurel a curious jolt. Not used to seeing him holding a baby, she felt as though she were seeing a completely new side to him. And, yes, she could see him, suddenly, as a loving father...

'Hi, Laurel.' He was the first to speak. 'I'm afraid we've got a few more cases on our hands. How are you?' There was a concerned softness in his tone that brought an emotional lump to her throat, although she doubted that the softness was all for her.

She cleared her throat. 'Exhausted actually...and I suspect it's only just begun.'

'We'll cancel all routine stuff—just concentrate on this epidemic, if that's what it is, and any other emergencies.' Jarrad's concise tones had the effect of pepping her up, of easing some of her anxiety about the sick babies. They had not yet had a death in Chalmers Bay at the clinic, and she didn't want anything to break that pattern if she could possibly help it.

'I feel a little less alone now that you're here,' she admitted truthfully. 'Thanks for getting back so quickly yesterday.'

'I'm glad you called me. Once the kids are stabilised we could get the air ambulance to come up, to take them and their mothers all at the same time. That would be best, I think.'

'Yes, I agree. What can I do right now?'

'Two of the younger babies need subcutaneous fluid lines put in immediately. I don't think we have time to poke around looking for veins until later,'

Jarrad said, looking at her levelly. 'I'm glad you're back.'

Over the next few days each twenty-four-hour period blended into a blur of activity for the staff at the medical station as they worked around the clock. There seemed to be a united, collective will-power in action as they strove to keep abreast of all that they had to do—a will-power to keep each baby alive.

As more babies had a diagnosis of meningitis definitely confirmed—with twelve confirmed cases by the end of the first week—Jarrad started a program of prevention in the community.

Any baby or young child who had the slightest upper respiratory infection would be brought in to the clinic to have a diagnostic throat swab taken. The swabs would be sent down to the city lab for analysis. In the meantime, each child would be started on a full course of antibiotics, using two types to cover all possibilities and to prevent the bacteria from becoming resistant to any one drug, which they had a tendency to do.

An air ambulance duly arrived in Chalmers Bay on the Saturday, complete with paramedic personnel, to take out the babies and their mothers, and every day more drugs came in by air. The staff took turns staying up at night. Laurel and Jarrad took turns sleeping.

As Laurel flung herself on her bed on the Friday night of the second week, having just kicked off her shoes and not bothered to undress, she knew that if things did not ease up soon she would collapse. When she closed her eyes she saw small bright lights, the proverbial stars shooting across her inner vision, and knew that she had been on the verge of fainting.

'You OK, Laurel?' Surprisingly, Jarrad was beside her, kneeling on the floor by her bed. 'I heard you groaning.' The skin of his face looked yellowish with fatigue, contrasting with the day's growth of dark beard. Lines were deep-etched around his eyes as he frowned down at her in concern.

'Oh. . .was I groaning?' Laurel murmured. 'I'm. . . just tired. That's all.'

When he gently stroked her face with his hand, pushing back stray strands of hair, it seemed the most natural thing in the world to her then, and just as natural that she should turn her head slightly to kiss his hand. It seemed to her that he needed comfort just as much as she did. 'When is it all going to end?' she whispered.

'Another week, maybe. . .it should ease up then,' he comforted her softly. Then he kissed her, placing his lips warmly on hers. Reaching up, she put her arms around his neck to pull him close to her, kissing him back with all the pent up need that she had suppressed since their argument. At that moment she didn't care what he or anyone else might think of her.

After a long moment, when she felt that she was sinking into a dark, velvety softness, he raised his mouth from hers and held her close in a tight hug that matched her own desperate clinging. 'Oh, Jarrad. . .' she said, her vulnerable emotions dangerously near the surface. 'Are we going to lose any of them. . .the babies?'

'I'm pretty sure not,' he said quietly, after a slight hesitation, his breath warm against her cheek. 'Tomorrow I think we should close down the medical station to all but dire emergencies and those needing injections, so that we can all get some rest and just concentrate on the infants. I think we can at last see the wood for the trees.'

This time she kissed him, moving her mouth the few inches to find his. In moments he was kissing her back in a quick flare of passion, stroking back her hair from her face in a tender yet proprietorial gesture that made Laurel feel weak with a hot wave of longing to make love to him completely, to hold the full length of his strong body against her own.

They both needed that comfort. There would be no reservations now. Yet she knew that this was not the time, even if it was very definitely the place. Any moment now, they would be called back to work.

Pulling back from him, feeling herself to be in a warm haze of an emotion that she had never experienced before, she looked into Jarrad's eyes to find an echo there of her own emotion. Then she knew with certainty that they had made a breakthrough of momentous proportions; whatever happened between them now, she knew instinctively that there would be no going back from this moment. And it had all happened so spontaneously. . .so wonderfully.

'Cup of tea? If I make it? Mmm?' he offered, smiling down at her with a rare warmth. Laurel had seen that warmth recently as he had comforted and hugged distraught mothers when they had wept with helpless fear beside the beds of their sick babies; she had seen it in the tenderness with which he had handled their small patients.

As she had watched him working competently, calmly, she had known that if anyone could keep death at bay, it would be him. Never again would she think him cool. Likewise, he had seen her tears, her fear and her strengths, over the past two weeks.

'Yes, please,' she agreed, stretching her arms up behind his shoulders. 'Who could pass up an offer like that!'

They released each other reluctantly. 'It feels so good to be on the receiving end of someone else's touch,' Laurel admitted wonderingly as she slid her hands down Jarrad's arms to rest them on her bed.

'After giving, giving, giving for so long. . .with little expectation of return except the satisfaction of the job, a relief that at least no one has died. . .yet.'

Jarrad raised his eyebrows at her in a comic, wry gesture that contrasted so much with his obvious exhaustion that she could barely restrain herself from flinging her arms around him.

'That's quite an admission, coming from you, Dr Harte,' he teased gently. 'An admission. . .in so many words. . .of vulnerability. Feet of clay, mmm? The efficient Dr Harte. . . Well, well! And would anyone's touch do, Laurel? Or dare I presume that only mine would serve the purpose?'

'Oh, only yours, Jarrad. Definitely,' she said provocatively, smiling. They both knew that under the teasing lightness there was a mutual, irrevocable seriousness. The sure knowledge gave Laurel a curious surge of rare joy. For a few dazed moments she felt as though she were standing outside herself, watching the unfolding of a drama that had an inevitable ending. Then, frightened to presume, she quickly brushed the image away.

'I'll get the tea,' Jarrad murmured soberly, getting to his feet. 'Before I begin to consider that as some sort of invitation.'

As she took the brief respite, cocooned in warmth while she waited for Jarrad to come back with the tea, Laurel mulled over all that had happened over the past two weeks. Somehow during that hectic time she, Jarrad, or Bonnie Mae had found a few minutes to make telephone calls to the city to check up on Rick Sommers, whose treatment had started, as well as Doug Rayner and John, who had had a further operation on his fingers to have the nerve supply improved.

They had also needed to find out about the babies who had been transported earlier, which they had done with a certain trepidation because not all the mothers had been able to leave Chalmers Bay to go with their babies. No member of the staff wanted to have to break the news of a death. So far, all had survived—all had made progress of one sort or another. That news had been gratifying, had helped to keep the staff going.

Life for Joe Fletcher had been hectic too—preparing food for staff at all hours, ferrying supplies from the airstrip and specimens such as throat swabs and blood in tubes the other way, so that they could be flown out. He seemed to thrive on the activity, never complained.

So far, so good. . .just.

CHAPTER EIGHT

As THE epidemic gradually declined the staff began to make more home visits to see babies and young children who had upper respiratory infections, to try to nip any further cases in the bud. Teenagers were vulnerable too, yet the staff had to take care not to give antibiotics indiscriminately, since resistance to them could be built up by certain bacteria so that they might no longer be effective in the future.

They were into the month of August now. As Laurel drove the pick-up truck around Chalmers Bay one morning she was suddenly mindful of the date, and the few weeks that she had left in the Arctic. Because they had all been working so hard recently, the time seemed to have gone by at a fantastic pace.

Looking now at the clear blue sky, at the landscape bright with sunlight, as she felt the warmth of the sun on the upper part of her lightly clad body, she felt that maybe she could stay in the Arctic for years, if only it would be like this for longer. She knew that it was a fool's paradise; by the end of August there would already be very definite intimations of winter on the way.

'Hi, Doc!' Someone called and waved to her as she passed, and she recognized the young man, Tommy Patychuk, to whom Bonnie Mae had introduced her some weeks before. He suffered mild, periodic asthma for which he came to the clinic from time to time.

Laurel waved back, smiling. She liked Tommy, as she liked most of the Inuit people with whom she had come in contact. Now Tommy was with his girlfriend, Anik.

Yes, she had mixed feelings about going back to 'civilisation', yet she knew that she would probably not cope well in the winter up here. Snow and bitter cold for eight months of the year was not her idea of heaven. Lying on a beach under a palm tree appealed to her much more.

Having seen a whole slew of children, Laurel decided to drop in on Josi Landers, who would no doubt offer her a very welcome cup of tea. She parked the pick-up truck beside Josi's small, neat, single-storey house that belonged to the national bank for whom Josi's husband worked.

Josi looked tired, yet bright and expectant when she opened the door, so that Laurel felt an immediate concern for this woman who was painfully thin as well. 'Hi, Dr Harte, I thought it would be you when I heard that old truck grinding along. It's good to see you. Come in.'

'How are you, Josi? You look a little more tired than usual.'

'Yes, I am. The reason is, we're actually going in two weeks' time! Isn't that great? I've exhausted myself making a start with the packing, trying to get everything wound up. Can't wait to get out of here, I can tell you!' She paused for breath, her eyes shining excitedly. 'There's going to be enough of the summer left when we get back down to Edmonton to have a decent holiday... We'll go to our vacation cottage, or we might just go out to the Rockies for a couple of weeks. Tea?'

'Please. I'm just gasping for a cup of tea—or two.' While Josi absented herself for a few minutes, still talking excitedly from her kitchen, Laurel looked around her at the open boxes and suitcases on the living-room floor, partially packed.

'Tell me how you're feeling, Josi. I shall want to keep your medical chart up to date, so that you can take a copy of the notes down to the city with you. I'd like to take your blood pressure and your temperature while I'm here. Have you been keeping a record yourself of your temperature?'

'I sure have! My husband said the other day that he's forgotten what I look like without a thermometer stuck in my mouth.' Josi laughed, coming in with two mugs of tea. 'He never was a guy for giving compliments.'

'He'll be glad to get out of here, and all. Not that people aren't nice...they've been really great. It's just that we like a different sort of life, you know—barbecues in the back yard, pool parties and all that. We'd go mad up here.'

'I know what you mean. I'll take your temperature and blood pressure before we have our tea, if you don't mind—get that out of the way.'

When Laurel was on her second mug of tea her beeper, which she kept clipped to the pocket of her trousers, emitted a series of quick, shrill beeps that made her and Josi jump. 'Well, I haven't been called on that thing for some time,' Laurel said, switching it off. 'That means that I'm wanted at the medical station. Could I use your phone, Josi?'

'We haven't got a phone here because we use the one at the bank. Just go through the back yard and you're in the bank. Go into Martin's office.'

'OK. Thanks a lot for the tea. I feel rejuvenated. I'll see you at the clinic next week. Let me know your flight date, Josi. I'll give you a good check-up before you finally go. You have all your appointment dates for Edmonton in a safe place?'

'I sure do! Bye for now, Dr Harte.'

A niggling worry entered Laurel's mind as she walked briskly across the small back yard and through a gate to the rear of the bank. Only once before had she been paged when she was on rounds in the community; otherwise someone else at the medical station had always been able to deal with any accidents or other emergencies until she had returned. Maybe they needed to operate right away and wanted her to give a general anaesthetic. She could not shake a growing premonition that all was not well.

Josi's husband, Martin, tactfully vacated his office in the bank so that she could make her call and have a private conversation. Only a few seconds elapsed before the call was answered and she heard Bonnie Mae's voice, unusually breathless and urgent.

'Laurel. . .? Thank God it's you! You'd better get back here pronto, and prepare yourself for a shock. I hate to tell you this over the phone, but Jarrad's been shot.' Bonnie Mae spoke the words in a clipped manner, breathing hard as though she had been running.

'Shot? Shot. . .? But. . .what do you mean? I don't. . .' Laurel stammered, thankful that she was alone, feeling a tingling sensation of shock.

'It's OK, he isn't dead,' Bonnie Mae said bluntly. 'But he's bleeding. A couple of drunks were brought in here by the RCMP to be stitched up—they'd been fighting. One of them pulled a hand-gun out of his boot in our outpatient department and fired it at the other guy. . . Didn't hit him. Jarrad got in the way.'

'Oh, no. . .no.' Laurel moaned the words helplessly.

'He's been hit in two places,' Bonnie Mae continued, talking at breakneck speed. 'The shoulder. . .I don't think it's low enough to be in the chest cavity, but we're not taking any chances. He's breathing OK so far, and Skip's taking X-rays right now. I've already been on to the airstrip to get them to hold the Edmonton flight this afternoon. Lucky for us, there's a flight due in just after noon.'

'Oh, my God...my God...where else is he hit?' Laurel gripped the telephone hard, as though it were a lifeline linking her to Jarrad.

'In the right thigh, high up,' Bonnie Mae said tensely. 'Judging by the state of his blood pressure, the slug went clean through the femoral artery—and he's bleeding bad. It came right out the other side, by the look of it. We'll have to do something about that pretty damn smart! I've got the pneumatic tourniquet on. We're getting the OR ready. How soon can you be back here?'

'A few minutes. I'm coming, Bonnie.' Her voice was anguished, 'Don't let anything happen to him.'

'I won't. Just get yourself here.'

Afterwards, in the truck, careering along the main road at the full capacity of the engine, Laurel did not remember leaving the bank or how she had got back to the vehicle. Gripping the steering wheel, her eyes fixed on the road ahead, she whispered Jarrad's name over and over again. Then she began to pray, scarcely realising what she was doing. 'Please... Oh, please, God, don't let him die...don't let him die.'

Laurel had never lacked imagination, and now she could see vividly in her mind the spectacle of Jarrad's body pouring blood from a severed femoral artery, his life literally flowing away. In that moment, with a powerful, irrefutable flash of a shocking insight, she realised that she loved Jarrad Lucas. And not with the immature, adoring love that she had felt for Max. No...a strong, unwavering, mature woman's love, for better or worse.

During that bone-jarring dash to the medical station—as other people and vehicles on the road got out of her way quickly when they recognised her truck and responded to the honking of her horn—she also knew, with a terrible certainty, that if Jarrad were to die now she would mourn him for the rest of her life.

The realisation was like a double blow to her. How could she operate on him? How could she have his death on her conscience, if he were to die because she could not cope? The thread between life and death was very fragile. How well she knew that!

'No. . .no. . .no. . .' The word screamed itself repeatedly in her consciousness, at her realisation of a profound love, as the professional part of her began to plan what she had to do. . .must do. 'Oh, please, God,' she whispered, 'help me. Give me the strength!'

Up to now, she had not realised what a good driver she was; fear made her intent and instinctively careful. If anything happened to her, there would be little hope for Jarrad—although she didn't doubt that Bonnie Mae and Skip would operate if they had to.

Visions of Max came to her then—a young, laughing Max. Then she saw him mangled on the highway in his wrecked car, as it had been described to her afterwards. Try as she might, she had never been able to dispel that nightmarish picture. Perhaps now it would be superseded by one of Jarrad, as she would find him on her arrival at the medical station. Perhaps she was fated to fall for men who met violent deaths. . .

She brought the truck to a skidding halt beside the entrance to the clinic. In moments she was running through the outpatient department towards the operating-room, knowing that Bonnie Mae would have Jarrad there, would be putting in intravenous lines, that Skip would be preparing to operate. They would be waiting for her.

As she ran past the ward area she saw Nuna and several of the mothers in there with the sick infants.

Thank God *that* was being taken care of!

In the change-room next to the OR she tore off her outer clothing with hands that were shaking with the effects of shock. She was shivering and out of breath as she pulled on a scrub suit, then put on an operating cap and face mask. A tightness took hold of her chest and throat as she came out. For the first time in her professional life as a surgeon she was frightened in a way that she had never been frightened before.

Jarrad was deathly pale—sure evidence that he was bleeding badly; that was the first thing she noticed after she had pushed open the double swing doors to the operating-room and walked quickly to the stretcher where he lay. Bonnie Mae had two intravenous lines going—one was delivering blood, the other a clear solution that Laurel soon saw was dextrose and saline—and Bonnie was adjusting the flow as she approached. Her eyes raked the screens of the computerised monitors.

'Sure glad you're here!' Bonnie Mae said in an undertone, gesturing towards a brief medical chart on which she had recorded Jarrad's vital signs. 'Take a look at that. Those are the readings I took before I got him hooked up to the monitor, before I got the IVs going. I'm running in the O negative blood—we've got plenty of that. We've also got plenty of plasma. The BP's steady right now. . .still pretty low.'

'That's really great, Bonnie. You've done wonders,' she commended the nurse, who certainly knew what she was doing.

Although she had kept her voice down, Jarrad opened his eyes and looked sideways. 'Laurel?' he said weakly, and the sound brought tears to Laurel's eyes.

'Yes, I'm here, Jarrad.' Unashamedly she let him see her crying; there was no point in hiding it. Bonnie Mae's eyes were red and puffy from having shed tears and Skip was scrubbed and frantically preparing instruments and sutures on his sterile set-up, subdued and silent.

'Sorry. . .' Jarrad whispered. 'Bloody stupid thing. . .' Their eyes met as she stood beside the stretcher, and something of his old rueful expression surfaced briefly as he saw her tears. 'Don't cry, my love. . .don't want you to be upset. . .'

'I can't operate, Jarrad. . .not on you,' she moaned despairingly, her face close to his as she bent over him. She closed her eyes briefly, to blot out his pale face. 'I couldn't take it, you see. . .'

It was not necessary to spell it out. During the agonising seconds in which they looked at each other it was clear in his face that he knew she would not be able to bear it if he were to die. At the same time they both knew that there was no alternative, that her words were pointless; if she did not operate, he would bleed to death anyway—and soon.

For those awful moments Laurel had no idea that she was twisting her hands together, agitatedly wringing them in despair, until Jarrad grasped both her hands in his and held them still.

'Tell me what you're going to do, Laurel, how you're going to go about it. Give me all the details.'

'Oh, Jarrad. . .' she whispered, feeling as though her heart would break, grasping his hands, returning his strong, reassuring grip. The pain in his eyes told her what an effort the action cost him as he leaned towards her. The thick dressings over the wound just below his right shoulder and those covering his thigh below the tourniquet were stained with blood.

'Look at me, Laurel,' he insisted quietly. 'Tell me.'

'I'll give you a spinal anaesthetic,' she said slowly, 'then I'll start on the leg. I'll make an incision, locate and clamp the bleeding artery, then I'll do what I can to repair it, using sutures and a graft. Then I'll clean and irrigate the wound, put in a drain and sew up. I might also put in some dye, take an X-ray. . .make sure I've got all the bleeders.'

'Go on. You're doing great.' His bloodshot tired eyes held a warmth of admiration, unmistakable as he listened to her.

'Then I. . .I'll have to have you transferred, of course. As for the shoulder wound. . .' She glanced quickly at the X-rays that were displayed on the wall panel. 'The bullet is still in there. I'm not going to try to dig it out—there won't be time. And since there appears to be minimal bleeding at that spot, I'll just irrigate the wound, replace the dressing and let the guys in the city have a go at that.'

'Good. . .good, I thoroughly approve,' he said, encouraging her. 'Do it then, Dr Harte. I have every faith in you. I trust you with my life.'

'Yes. . .I will do it. After all, this is my specialty—messing about with arteries!' she said, suddenly able to smile at him reassuringly as she gained confidence, even though her lips trembled as she returned the pressure of his hands. 'You're going to be fine! One thing I'm sure of—without you in this world, Jarrad, everything would turn instantly to dross. I couldn't let that happen!'

That was the nearest she could come now to telling him that she loved him. Releasing his hands gently, she moved away, leaving him to make of it what he would. 'Are you ready, Skip?' she added, looking over to where Skip was tearing open packets of sutures. 'And you, Bonnie?'

'I'm ready, Dr Harte,' Skip answered calmly.

'Yes, ma'am!' Bonnie Mae said as she opened up the sterile tray for the spinal anaesthetic. 'In a constant state of readiness, that's me!'

'I'll need some Demerol first,' Laurel said to Bonnie Mae as she quickly gathered equipment together on the anaesthetic cart, feeling herself moving into the swing of things. 'And I'll need to have some heparin handy for when I put in the arterial graft, once I've got the artery clamped, to prevent unwanted clotting. Have to go easy on that, though, since he's bleeding in the shoulder.'

'Yeah. It's all right here, on the anaesthetic cart,' Bonnie Mae said. 'And by the way, the guys at the airstrip will be holding the flight for as long as necessary. No sweat there!'

'Great!' Laurel said. The feeling of sick dread had given way to a professional calm when she took a sterile hypodermic syringe and needle from the anaesthetic cart in order to draw up the painkilling drug. Her movements were quick, purposeful, professional, her hands as steady as a rock.

When that was done, she went back over to the stretcher on which Jarrad lay. 'I'm going to give you some Demerol in the IV line, Jarrad,' she said, striving to keep a tremor out of her voice. 'Then we'll get on with the spinal. I'll talk to you when it's all finished.'

Then she pulled down her face mask and kissed him on the forehead. His skin felt cool and clammy. Words from *Hamlet* came to her mind: 'Good-night, sweet prince, And flights of angels sing thee to thy rest!'

She mentally pushed aside a dark foreboding as she prepared to inject the contents of the syringe directly into the intravenous line near its point of entry at the back of Jarrad's hand. Hamlet had been dead when those words were spoken. She was not going to let Jarrad die.

'I trust you implicitly,' he said, his eyes intently on her, as though he wanted her to be his last vision before the powerful drug forced his eyes closed. Laurel alternately watched Jarrad's face and the plunger of the syringe as she slowly pushed the drug into the intravenous line. Behind her there was intense, quiet activity from Bonnie Mae and Skip.

Peace came over Jarrad's face as his muscles relaxed and his eyelids closed. The Demerol would take his pain away, would make him sleep deeply but not actually anaesthetise him; it would be enough that they would be able to turn him on his side to insert a needle for the spinal anaesthetic, which would anaesthetise the lower part of his body so that they could operate on the thigh. For the injured shoulder she would later inject a local anaesthetic.

'OK, guys!' Bonnie Mae said, in a firm, mustering tone that she referred to as her best hog-calling voice. 'Let's move it!'

'Release the tourniquet very slowly please, Bonnie,' Laurel said as she peered intently inside the deep incision in Jarrad's leg that Skip held wide open with metal retractors, and she adjusted the powerful operating light so that she could see the blood vessels very clearly.

A few moments ago she had clamped the femoral artery that she could see had been torn by the bullet and had been leaking blood at a rapid pace. She had used the suction apparatus very carefully to clear blood from the wound. 'I want to check that the major veins haven't been hit, as well as some of the lesser arteries,' she had explained to Skip.

'OK. . .put the tourniquet on again, Bonnie, for a few minutes, and time it, please,' she said later. 'Pass me the Dacron arterial graft, Skip, and the 4.0 mersilene suture. . . We'll get the femoral artery fixed up so that we'll get a proper blood supply to the leg again.'

There was mostly silence in the operating-room,

each staff member intent on doing their assigned job, straining for the last iota of concentration and expertise. Bonnie Mae alternated between standing at the head of the operating table to check Jarrad's vital signs and assisting with anything that Laurel or Skip needed for the operation. The monitors recorded the blood pressure and pulse rate automatically; Bonnie Mae had only to chart them. She was watching them intently at all times.

The three of them were only too aware that if Jarrad did not survive they would blame themselves. As one bag of blood emptied Bonnie Mae hung up another, and connected it to the intravenous line. From time to time Laurel glanced at the monitors.

'So far, so good, eh?' Bonnie Mae murmured, peering over to see what Laurel was doing.

'Yes,' Laurel agreed feelingly. 'Keep your fingers crossed.'

'I'm praying, don't you worry!' Bonnie Mae said meaningfully. 'Praying like hell!'

'I'll want to turn him on his side later, Bonnie, to irrigate the exit wound of the bullet and put a drain in there. I'll need warm saline and hydrogen peroxide for that, please. Later, I'll irrigate the shoulder wound as well.'

A considerable time later, the external telephone rang in the operating-room, bringing them all back to a sudden awareness that there was an outside world.

'It's the airstrip,' Bonnie Mae announced when she had answered it. 'The Edmonton plane's in already. They'll hold the outgoing flight for us as long as it takes. . .they just want a rough idea of how long we'll be.'

Laurel looked at the wall clock. 'Tell them that we can be at the airstrip in three quarters of an hour.'

'Do you want me to go with him to Edmonton,

Laurel?' Bonnie Mae asked after she had hung up. 'In my view, it might be better if I went, so at least we've got one doctor here.' Although she did not add that the trip would be a tremendous strain on Laurel because of how she felt about Jarrad, the subtle awareness was there in Bonnie Mae's voice.

Laurel smiled at her tiredly. Bonnie Mae was no fool. You could not work closely with two people for weeks without having a pretty good idea of how they felt about each other, in spite of arguments, disagreements and other negative emotions that surfaced from time to time. 'Yes, that would probably be the best,' she agreed quietly. 'You're much more familiar with the system than I am. I'll come with you to the airstrip to see you off, of course.'

They could hardly leave the medical station without a doctor, and although she would be in a state of acute anxiety about Jarrad until he was safely in a hospital of some repute, she knew that on a flight there would be little more she could do that Bonnie Mae could not also do. As Jarrad had said of her, so she could also say of Bonnie Mae—'I trust you implicitly.'

'Great!' Bonnie Mae said. 'I always keep a bag packed. All I have to do is grab that, and one of the emergency kits, and I'm all set to go. I'll call you the minute I'm inside the airport down there. I've got an ambulance meeting the plane, and the hospital knows he's coming. I'll stay down there at least overnight, at the NMDC house.'

'That's great, Bonnie,' Laurel agreed.

As they prepared to bring the operation to a successful conclusion Laurel was aware that just about every muscle in her body ached. Then she remembered that Jarrad had called her 'my love'. It was a verbal talisman that she would cling to in the dark days ahead.

* * *

Jarrad was groggy but awake when they arrived at the airstrip in the Royal Canadian Mounted Police's truck-ambulance, driven by Greg Farley. The intravenous lines were still going, and would be kept running for the duration of the flight. Laurel, Bonnie Mae and the other RCMP officer, Wayne Keeling, sat in the back with Jarrad on a stretcher.

Jarrad had taken Laurel's hand for the short journey there—as much, she suspected, to comfort her as to garner some comfort for himself. Distraught, yet outwardly calm, she could not trust herself to speak. Her face felt stiff and her clenched jaw ached from the effort of maintaining composure. She knew that her eyes were glazed with unshed tears.

'What happened to those two guys who had the gun?' Bonnie Mae asked Wayne Keeling in an undertone just as the truck pulled up at the main entrance to the airstrip. 'I didn't see what you did with them.'

'Both in the slammer,' Wayne said, with obvious grim satisfaction. 'As far as I'm concerned, they can rot there! We sure ain't gonna let those guys out in a hurry. The one who did the shooting will definitely be charged with attempted murder.'

'Good! I get pretty sick of these trigger-happy guys, waving guns about like they were water pistols, or something,' Bonnie Mae answered back.

'Yeah. . .'

The jet, waiting to take off for Edmonton, seemed to dwarf the small, single-storey air terminal building. In-flight personnel were waiting to accompany the stretcher over the tarmac. 'Well, you sure got a good plane,' Wayne Keeling commented. 'That's gonna make real good time down there.'

They all walked alongside the stretcher as it was wheeled to the steps of the aircraft, then the top was lifted off the frame to be carried up the steps.

'You couldn't have more attention if you were royalty, Dr Lucas,' Bonnie Mae quipped. 'Better take a good, deep breath of fresh Arctic air. Before you know it you'll be breathing in traffic fumes.'

'My thanks to all of you...' Jarrad said as he smiled and looked up at the clear Arctic sky, before the two RCMP officers and two of the male crew members hoisted the stretcher up the first step to the aircraft.

Laurel still could not trust herself to speak; there was a tightness in her throat and her eyes were stinging. She intended to say goodbye to him when he was installed inside. They had done all they could for him in Chalmers Bay.

'Laurel.' Jarrad took her hand again when the stretcher was safely strapped into position inside the aircraft. 'I'll call you from down there, as soon as I can get my hands on a telephone.' His voice came out in a croak, and he moistened his dry lips repeatedly with his tongue, as though each word were painful to him. The pressure of his hand on hers served to remind her even more poignantly that he was soon to be taken away from her.

'Yes.' Laurel found her voice. 'Make sure you do. Don't forget. I'll be waiting.'

There was hurried activity all around them as other passengers and luggage came aboard. Jarrad pulled Laurel down so that she was squatting beside him, his eyes commanding her to look at him. 'Thank you for what you've done...you saved my life. I'll never forget it...how could I?'

There was a wealth of meaning in his words; they contained apology for past misunderstandings, respect, admiration...and love, even. Laurel clung to those words, like the proverbial drowning man clutching at a straw.

'I doubt that I'll be coming up here again,' he went

on slowly, thoughtfully. 'There wouldn't be much point, since we haven't much time left. Sorry to leave you in the lurch like this...'

'That doesn't matter,' she murmured, not knowing how to bear the imminent goodbye. Absently and compulsively, she stroked his hair back from his pale forehead. 'You take care... Words are so inadequate, aren't they? I've sweated blood for you, Jarrad...or at least it feels like it—so you take damn good care of yourself, and do exactly what Bonnie Mae tells you to do. OK? You'll be all right now.'

Although she spoke lightly, it was an effort; it took all her concentration to prevent her face from showing the abject grief that consumed her. The knowledge that he would survive was the only thing that prevented her from breaking down.

'Sure!' His lips stretched in a faint smile, his face lighting up momentarily. 'With Bonnie, one doesn't have a choice. I've been thinking...if you hadn't had that job with Josh, you would probably not have known how to do such a good job on a severed artery. God...or fate...works in mysterious ways.'

'Yes...there are too many "ifs". Better not to dwell on them.'

'There's something I've been wanting to say to you for some time.' Jarrad gripped her hand harder as he frowned with tired concentration, as his eyes met hers with a strange urgency. 'If you spend too much time...too much psychic energy...in trying to put the past right, you neglect to live in the present...to do the right thing. The world moves on. I've found that out in my own life, and I think that's what you're doing, Laurel. Don't let it happen. You're such a lovely woman...'

'Oh, Jarrad, for God's sake...' she said brokenly, lowering her head for a few seconds onto his shoulder, not pretending that she didn't know exactly what he was talking about. And was this his way of answering her indirect declaration of love?

'I'll see you again, Laurel,' he whispered. 'Don't cry, sweetheart. Goodbye.'

This time she kissed him on a cheek that she had wet with her tears, and he moved so that his mouth brushed hers briefly. 'Goodbye, Jarrad,' she whispered. 'Good luck.' Then she stood up, keeping her head bent as she surreptitiously wiped her tears.

Bonnie Mae busied herself fixing up the two bags of IV fluids on a portable pole, making sure the lines were not twisted. 'Good luck, Bonnie,' Laurel said, straightening up. 'Thanks for everything. I couldn't have managed without you. You were absolutely wonderful.'

'I'll take good care of him—don't you worry about a thing,' Bonnie Mae said huskily, her plump face set in lines of very definite intent. She wore a voluminous padded nylon jacket over her pink uniform trouser suit, and her short brown hair, usually hidden under an operating cap, curled attractively round her face; she looked very capable. This was all in a day's work for her, Laurel knew—as Bonnie herself was fond of pointing out.

She and Bonnie gave each other a hug, which had many unspoken communications in it, then, with another quick backward glance at Jarrad, she pushed her way off the plane, knowing that he was watching her retreating back. Letting the tears run freely now, she walked across the runway to the RCMP truck that would give her a ride back to the medical station.

Already Chalmers Bay had changed for her; in the space of a few hours it had become an isolated, lonely place. Jarrad was already in a no-man's-land on the aircraft, as was Bonnie Mae. Soon they would be gone and she would feel very alone at the medical station, even though there was a strong sense of community in Chalmers Bay itself.

'Don't you worry, Dr Harte,' Wayne Keeling said as she clambered up into the truck. 'He's in good hands. If anyone can keep him alive, it's Bonnie Mae. What I haven't seen her do isn't worth talking about! What you want is a stiff drink. Have you got anything back there?'

'Yes. . .we've got some brandy.'

'Great! You make yourself a cup of black tea, add a good slug of the brandy and plenty of sugar. That'll set you up.' Wayne started the engine and they were off on the pot-holed road.

Back at the medical station, the staff annexe seemed deathly quiet after the receding noise of the RCMP truck had finally died away. Laurel slowly took off her jacket and hung it on a peg. Automatically she went to the kitchen to plug in the electric kettle, to get herself out a mug to make tea and to forage in a cupboard for the bottle of brandy.

While she was waiting for the water to boil she wandered disconsolately into Jarrad's room through the partially open door. The bed was untidy and the room looked pleasantly lived-in; he had flung a sweater over the end of the bed as though he would, in a few minutes, come out of the bathroom to put it on. Laurel began to sob then, a bitter, poignant keening of grief—uncontrollable.

Confusedly, she knew that she was crying for the loss of Jarrad, for her intense anxiety about him, and because of her newly realised love that he did not know about; she was also crying for Max Freer, for the way he had been as a young medical student, before he had become hardened and arrogant. She was saying goodbye to Max for ever, goodbye to her first youth, to the naïve girl she had been. For now she was inevitably changed. Jarrad had been right; she had been preoccupied, to an obsessive degree, with painful, unfinished business.

She lay down on Jarrad's bed, turning her face into the pillow that was faintly scented with the subtle, expensive aftershave lotion that he wore. Often she had tried to divine what was in it. . .ginger, lime, cloves, orange blossom. . .exotic things from warm places. Her hands clenched the soft material in an agony of loss. That she loved him, with an intense, passionate love, was no longer in doubt. Was it possible that he loved her? The agonised question echoed repeatedly in her muddled brain.

Then there was Ginny. . .the mysterious, but very real and very beautiful Ginny. After her experiences of Max's unfaithfulness, could she trust another man who already had a woman in the wings? But common sense told her that if Ginny had been someone special to Jarrad, he would hardly have left her to work in a remote place for months with a female colleague.

Laurel rolled onto her back and looked up dully at the ceiling. Perhaps she would not see Jarrad again; the possibility had to be faced, and she faced it now. Any contact between them would have to be very deliberate, by mutual choice in this vast country, even though he had said, 'I'll see you again, Laurel.'

He had not told her where he would be working after Chalmers Bay, if he even knew himself—although he knew where and when she would be starting her new job. Mid-October was the date that she had been given for the start of her orientation period at the new hospital.

Forcing herself to get up, she went to the kitchen to make tea. There would have to be some sort of official inquiry about the shooting, of course, which would also take time. Laurel was glad that she had not been a witness, although no doubt she would have to make a detailed report about Jarrad's injuries and treatment.

Wayne Keeling was right; sweet tea without milk and with a good measure of brandy was great for soothing one's anxieties, she decided as she stood leaning against a wall in the sitting-room to drink it, waiting, her hands cupped around the hot mug. She could not bring herself to sit, to pretend that she could relax yet.

At some point, in a few days, she would have to pack up Jarrad's belongings, arrange to have them sent by air to Edmonton before he was discharged from the hospital there.

Then she heard what she had been waiting for, straining her hearing, feeling a renewed sense of utter loneliness. In the silence of the annexe the muffled distant roar of the jet taking off from the airstrip came to her. Unreservedly she let the tears flow until there was no emotion left in her other than a deep, paralysing sense of sadness.

Then she put through a call to Skip to make sure that everything was all right, that Nuna was there with the few remaining babies they had recovering from meningitis, that they had no emergency cases pending. Next, she put through a call to the office of the Northern Medical Development Corporation in Yellowknife, to inform them that her colleague had been shot and that she would like a replacement as soon as possible.

'I would like you to consider,' she added at the end, surprising herself, 'the possibility of my leaving Chalmers Bay two weeks before my time is up, or even earlier. This has all been a great shock to me... If you could consider getting someone else to replace me, also, I would appreciate it.'

They agreed, commiserating with her. 'Funny,' Laurel said aloud as she stood staring at the telephone after she had replaced the receiver, 'I didn't know I was going to say that...'

Then she went to her room and slept.

CHAPTER NINE

WHEN the call came from Bonnie Mae, hours later, Laurel was ready for it, keyed up and waiting, her mood having hardened to one of a sober, subdued grief. As usual in such circumstances, she would deal with it as best she could, then use up her surplus energy in work. At least in Chalmers Bay there was no shortage of that.

'I'm in the Edmonton airport,' Bonnie Mae announced, talking loudly against the background noise. 'Can't talk for long, Laurel, we've got to get moving—the ambulance guys are waiting for me. Jarrad's fine. I thought you'd want to know that right away. He slept for most of the flight; I kept him topped up with Demerol. His blood pressure's fine—no obvious bleeding. So it looks as though you did a great job!'

'Thank God!' Laurel breathed, a wave of abject relief washing over her, leaving her elated and lightheaded. 'That's wonderful! Thank you, Bonnie. . . thanks for everything. Keep in touch. . .and, Bonnie, give my love to Jarrad. . .please.'

'Sure will! He said to tell you that he's missing you already, and that you're the chief now. He said you would understand!' Bonnie Mae gave a loud cackle of laughter. 'If there's any change, Laurel, I'll call you later tonight. Otherwise, I'll call you tomorrow when I know my return flight—don't think I'll come back till the day after tomorrow; I'm absolutely bushed! Besides, I want to know what's going on with Jarrad before I leave.' She paused for breath.

Hearing the disembodied noises from the far-off airport, Laurel was more than ever acutely and poignantly aware of her isolation. 'I wish I could be there with you, Bonnie,' she said wistfully. 'You take as long as you need down there—get rested. Everything's fine here. Take care.'

All elective surgery was cancelled until further notice, unless very minor. The next day Laurel left Skip in charge of the medical station and took the pick-up truck around Chalmers Bay, starting early, to check up on some of their previous meningitis babies and on those who had shown signs of infection earlier and were receiving antibiotics. The first batch of babies who had been transferred to the city were now coming back in ones and twos on any available flight.

Not stopping for lunch, calling in to the clinic from time to time, she was determined to see every baby who needed to be seen; there was a sense of urgency about it now, a sense of wanting to get everything wrapped up satisfactorily before a new doctor came to join her—before she was herself ready to leave. Fortunately, so far, there had been no deaths.

The zenith of the short Arctic summer had come and gone, though flowers were still blooming underfoot on the tundra, birds were rearing their young and white Beluga whales cavorted in the cold waters of Coronation Gulf. Before the migration of the birds and animals, she would be gone herself.

As Laurel drove purposefully around the community she was conscious of enjoying the sweet, pure air, the quiet surroundings of the village, the unique land that stretched as far as she could see when she went to the edge of the community, where the habitat of man came to an abrupt end.

Skip was waiting for her with a message when she got back in the afternoon. 'Dr Dan McCormick called from Calgary,' he said as soon as she walked through to the clinic area. 'He said that he's been asked by the NMDC if he could come up here for a while until the next guys are due partway through September, so I said you'd call him back, Dr Harte. He wants to know all about what happened to Dr Lucas. He's a great guy—he comes up here a lot.'

'They don't waste any time, do they? I don't suppose it's really up to me—the final decision, that is. Thanks, Skip. As soon as I've had something to eat and drink I'll call him. Anything doing here?'

'Just a few people in for changes of dressings. I can cope with that.'

There was a certain solace in being in the quiet annexe later, to have time to think, although Jarrad's empty room seemed to mock her with an evocation of unvoiced longings as she busied herself with the homely task of preparing a simple meal. Jarrad's absence was like the death of part of herself. But he would be all right now; she did not doubt that.

As she prepared the meal she rehearsed what she was going to say to Dr Dan McCormick and how she was going to ask his advice about getting a second doctor to replace her. The conviction was growing by the hour that she did not want to work in Chalmers Bay without Jarrad. Better just to get out and leave two new people to take over.

'I can be there in four days' time, if that's OK with you,' Dr Dan McCormick said cheerfully when she called him later at his office in Calgary, Alberta. 'I have a few things to wrap up here, then my partners can take over. We have a general practice here. I won't need to stay at the annexe—I stay with a ladyfriend in the town.'

'I really appreciate it,' Laurel said. 'I'm relieved, too, that I'm getting an old hand to come up. Did the

NMDC say anything to you about replacing me before my time is up? This shooting has been such a shock, I feel I'd like to get out sooner than I'd planned... have a holiday.'

'They're working on it,' he said. 'You'll know before I get up there, I expect. They're pretty good at getting you out when you want to go. Tell me about what happened to Dr Lucas.'

For some time they talked about the shooting, then about the meningitis epidemic, which was now definitely fizzling out. 'I feel much better having talked to you, Dan,' Laurel admitted. 'Thank you again for agreeing to come.'

'Oh, don't thank me,' he laughed. 'I like coming up there. I'm trying to persuade the lady to marry me! Maybe she'll be willing to set a date this time.'

'If there's anything I can do to expedite matters, just let me know,' Laurel said warmly, knowing that she was going to like working with Dan McCormick.

'I'll call you as soon as I know my flight up there. Goodbye for now.'

Bonnie Mae arrived back on the evening of the following day. Joe Fletcher drove to the airstrip to meet her flight, then brought her back to the annexe to have supper with Laurel and to discuss Jarrad's condition and the arrangements for his replacement. Laurel also broke the news to Bonnie that she wanted to go herself.

'I can't go on here without Jarrad—I don't know why,' she said. 'Everything seems to have lost all relevance without him.'

They were sitting across from each other at the dining-table, drinking some of the wine that Bonnie Mae had brought with her from the city, which went very well with the excellent meal that Joe had produced for them. Bonnie Mae looked momentarily startled.

'I can't say I really blame you,' she said, 'It's been very unsettling for all of us. You're sick with worry about him, and that's absolutely understandable.'

'Yes...and it isn't so much that,' Laurel said hesitantly, then swallowed a mouthful of food and wondered how she could explain something that she was not even sure about herself. 'It's just that... well...'

'You love him, don't you?' Bonnie Mae said, fixing her with that shrewd, assessing look that she gave to patients who were lying about their symptoms or their alcohol consumption.

'Yes...'

'Does he know?'

'No. At least, I haven't told him. I think maybe I'm the last woman he would want to love him. He doesn't generally go for women like me,' she said quietly.

'And what's that?'

'Ambitious professional women—what he would call calculating...'

'You're not calculating!' Bonnie Mae said vehemently. 'I'd say you're pretty soft, and if he doesn't know that by now, he ought to! And I think an ambitious professional woman is just what he does want.

'In my experience, and from observing other people, I'd say that men generally want a woman who is on the same level of intelligence as they are themselves, with not too much discrepancy between their mutual accomplishments...on a permanent basis, that is. And I guess we're talking permanent here?'

'Yes...' There was no point in prevaricating.

'Sure we are! There's something about this place that makes people come to terms with the basic realities of their lives, makes them confront themselves. Some people are scared of that...as scared as hell. Maybe he's one of them. Maybe you are too.'

Bonnie Mae heaved herself to her feet to go to the kitchen and fetch the apple pie that Joe had made for them. 'I have a very strong feeling that this shooting will make both of you confront those issues. Want some apple pie?'

'Please,' Laurel said distractedly.

Bonnie Mae hacked at the pie. 'Look at me and Chuck. . .' she said. 'We've known each other for years—been married in all but name. Now we're getting married in October because the time's right; we feel ready. Maybe the time's right for you two, and all. You just stay in touch with Jarrad Lucas, and maybe he'll realise it. My bet is that he's realised it already. When he was lying there bleeding like a stuck pig he must have been thanking his lucky stars that he had you!'

'I'm going to miss you, Bonnie. You're good for me. Except when it comes to food—that's enough pie for three people, if that's all for me!' She laughed as for the first time in days she felt a lifting of her spirits.

'I'm going to miss you too,' Bonnie Mae said, scraping some of the pie back into the dish. 'You'll come to my wedding, though, won't you? In Edmonton? I'm inviting you, and Dr Lucas. . .and anyone who's ever worked at this medical station. It'll be the best damn party you've ever been to!'

'Just try to keep me away!'

There was plenty of time for reflection on the flight out of Chalmers Bay to Edmonton two weeks later. So much had happened during those weeks, and Laurel knew she really needed those flight hours of forced inactivity to begin the long winding-down process that would bring her somewhere near a sense of relaxation.

Jarrad's belongings had been packed up and sent

down to the house in Edmonton that was for the use of Chalmers Bay medical staff and their patients and families when necessary, which was where she was heading herself, en route to Gresham.

She had had a quick, reassuring telephone call from Jarrad on the night of his arrival at the Edmonton hospital, then a letter had come from him, delivered by courier, only four days after she had operated on him; it had been written with a shaky hand as he had lain in a hospital bed after having had the bullet removed from his shoulder by another operation.

It had been a short letter, expressing gratitude to her and Bonnie Mae and Skip, telling her what had happened since his arrival at the hospital there and saying that he was well. Briefly, he'd mentioned that he hoped to go away somewhere hot to recuperate when he was discharged from hospital.

Reading and rereading the letter, Laurel had not been able to get over the feeling that he was not telling her everything, that this was perhaps a letter of goodbye—even taking into consideration the fact that he had been under stress as well as sedation when he had written it. She could not have said why she'd felt that way; there had just been something about it.

That feeling had increased her sense of urgency to get out of Chalmers Bay, even though her first anxiety about him had been calmed. Despite the many calls she had made to the city, she had been able to speak to him only twice, when he had sounded tired and sedated, so she had not questioned him much. Two days before her departure she had telephoned the city hospital to find out if Jarrad was still there, not having heard from him and had been told that he'd been discharged and had already left the country to go to Mexico to recuperate. The need to see Jarrad again, soon, was overwhelming; it dominated all her waking thoughts, filling her with a restless urgency.

Everything had happened very quickly to expedite her departure from Chalmers Bay, so that now, sitting on the plane, she could scarcely believe that she had said goodbye to Bonnie Mae, Skip, Nuna and Joe Fletcher—all of whom she had come to like very much, to view as friends. She would miss the RCMP officers too, and all the other people she had met. Many of them she would meet again at Bonnie Mae's wedding.

A lot of her patients had flown ahead of her to Edmonton, so in a sense she was getting a chance to check up on them by following them; it would be easier in the city to telephone the medical consultants who had taken over her patients, to find out what progress they were making. Josi Landers had just left, and Rick Sommers had been undergoing radiotherapy for some time, and had called the medical station himself to let them know how he was doing.

Although there was the inevitable feeling that she was leaving unfinished business, the bulk of her patients had been transferred out, and Dr Dan McCormick, a red-haired, cheerful man of Scottish extraction, had been almost eager to take over, while she herself had been replaced temporarily by a general surgeon also from Calgary, who had been up there before.

The first two things she noticed about the city airport were the noise and the smells of fuel and exhaust, then her vision was assaulted by the numbers of people milling around, waiting to go through to the arrivals area to pick up luggage.

Laurel found herself borne along by the crowd as she quickly tried to shift her mental processes, which would help her to adjust from the quiet sense of community that had prevailed in the isolation of Chalmers Bay to the jostling anonymity of the crowded city.

'Hello, Dr Harte, it's good to see you. I was wondering when you'd be down this way.' Rick Sommers shook hands with Laurel the next day as they stood in Dr Michael Leyton's private office. He was the doctor to whom she had referred Rick and Josi Landers. 'As you can see, I'm looking a little different from when you last saw me.'

Laurel was wearing a borrowed white lab coat over her ordinary clothing, in order to look more professional. 'Yes, you certainly are!' Laurel agreed enthusiastically. Dr Leyton had given her all the relevant details of Rick's treatment before Rick had come in, telling her that the radiotherapy had shrunk the tumour in his neck considerably.

Looking at Rick now, she could see what he meant. To someone who had not seen Rick before, the tumour would probably not even be discernible. She could only see the scar from where she had taken the biopsy because she knew where to look. 'It's remarkable,' she added. 'How are you feeling generally?'

'I feel good,' he said. 'I'm working full-time—the oil company has given me a job that's part desk-job and part out in the field. It suits me just fine, so I can come in for treatment when I have to.'

The rest of the day went quickly for Laurel. By the time she had also seen Josi Landers at Dr Leyton's office, then done some necessary shopping for herself, nothing remained for her to do in the city but have an evening meal and organise her luggage for departure the next day. She had done as much as she could do for her patients.

* * *

The next day Laurel found that Gresham airport was considerably more crowded than Edmonton airport had been, adding to her acute sense of disorientation at being back in the big outside world as she pushed her loaded luggage cart out into the arrivals lounge and automatically scanned the expectant faces of those people come to meet travellers—although she was not expecting to be met. No one in Gresham knew that she was arriving.

So it was unexpected, to say the least, when she heard her name being called as she moved out into the crowd. Peering round, she saw someone waving to her from a few yards away. Rather dazedly, to her amazement, she recognised none other than Dr Joshua Kapinsky coming towards her, pushing his way through with some difficulty.

'Hi. . . Laurel!' He was grinning at her and waving.

As she watched him coming towards her Laurel had a few revelatory seconds of absolute mental clarity, as though she were seeing him for the first time. The months in Chalmers Bay and the fact that he was no longer her boss and colleague had somehow brought a very necessary distancing. Had there been any remaining doubts in her mind about refusing his offer of marriage, they were dispelled now.

With the insight that separation sometimes brought, she saw him as he was—a prematurely aged man, tired, grey, overworked, who had little time in his life for anyone or anything other than the one thing he was good at—being a cardiac surgeon.

The realisation brought a sharp stab of pity for him, and an almost maternal commiseration with him for the lost time that he could never make up. . .at least, not with her. She knew with certainty then that if she were to marry him she too would be relegated to the sidelines of his life once the novelty of having a wife had worn off for him. Besides, she didn't love him. . .

Something that Jarrad had said to her came to mind—'Don't you want a normal life?' he had said. . . or words to that effect. Joshua Kapinsky could not offer her a 'normal' life, she knew that instinctively; not the sort of life that she was becoming to understand as normal. Somehow Jarrad had made her aware of it.

'How did you know I was coming?' she asked as Joshua reached her with outstretched hands. 'It's. . . so nice to be met.' And it was nice, she did not have to lie about that, even though her heart was sinking at the knowledge that she had a severe task ahead in order to tell him the truth.

'I have ways and means of finding out.' He grinned at her, the old cocksure Josh. 'I simply called that nurse, Bonnie Mae, who, as you must be aware, knows everything!'

In Joshua's car she did not have to worry about any awkwardness. He chatted continuously about things that had been going on at University Hospital in Gresham, and in the city in general, displaying little curiosity about the life she had led in Chalmers Bay— as though she had simply been away for a short break and would now pick up her life as before, with him as part of it.

He's got another think coming, Laurel vowed silently, with a touch of a rather grim amusement that held tinges of sadness, trying to plan just how she would prick the bubble of his self-absorption.

Distance had enabled her to see how self-important he had always been with her. Now that he was no longer her senior colleague, her boss, in effect, he had little hold over her; the relief of that was tremendous. Only now was it obvious how constraining the relationship had been.

Thoughts of Jarrad persistently invaded her mind.

Several hours later, over a superb four-course dinner served by his housekeeper out on a covered patio at the back of Joshua's sprawling, split-level house, in the balmy air of the late summer evening, she told him her decision.

CHAPTER TEN

'HELLO, Dr Harte. It is Dr Harte. . .isn't it?' The male voice hailing her in the entrance lobby of Riverton General Hospital on a Monday morning in October caused Laurel to pause in her purposeful stride. A man was standing at the reception desk, leaning on it, half turned towards her—a middle-aged man who looked vaguely familiar.

Her mind was very much preoccupied with the staff meeting that lay ahead, which would give her a chance to meet her medical colleagues is this new hospital where she was to work, and to introduce herself as well.

'Mr Foley! Isn't it?' she said incredulously after a moment, stopping beside him. 'What are you doing here in Riverton?'

The man looked so well, with a healthy-looking summer tan on his face, his skin fleshed out, that she hardly recognised him as the very sick man who had had a cardiac arrest at University Hospital in Gresham, although she thought it diplomatic not to say so.

'We've moved to Riverton, me and the wife, to be near our daughter who lives here.' Mr Foley smiled, gratified by her reaction. 'I come up here for a check-up once in a while. . .and we're not that far from Gresham if I need anything high-powered.'

'You look absolutely wonderful, Mr Foley. It's really great to see you,' Laurel enthused.

'I am wonderful! That bypass operation did the trick for me.'

They spent several minutes talking about his condition and about Laurel's months in Chalmers Bay. When she finally excused herself, Laurel realised that she would be late for the meeting if she didn't rush. Seeing Mr Foley again so unexpectedly made her feel as though she were moving in some sort of time warp, as though Chalmers Bay had never really existed for her, had all been a dream.

Breathlessly she arrived at the rather cramped meeting room, which was on the ground floor of the hospital, overlooking the extensive gardens. Chairs were placed round an enormous oval table in the centre of the room. Someone indicated the chair that had been allotted to her and she sat down, picking up the papers of the agenda.

While many city hospitals were having to close beds because of decreasing funds, this hospital had been favoured with government money for expansion, following the exodus of many city dwellers to this smaller, less expensive community that was surrounded by farmland.

'Help yourself to coffee.' The middle-aged doctor who sat next to her indicated the flasks of coffee that were on the table in front of them. 'And since you won't have time to read that agenda before we start, I'll give it to you in a nutshell. We're going to discuss the expansion of the hospital, the taking on of new medical staff—including the introduction of a new chief of surgery—and the opening of a new rheumatology department.' He grinned at her. 'Not too exciting, eh?'

'About average, as meetings go.' Laurel smiled back as she helped herself to coffee and looked rather shyly around the room at her fellow doctors who were soon to be her colleagues.

Sitting at the head of the table was the chairman of the meeting, Dr Wilf Crayford, the present chief of surgery, who had interviewed her for her job and who was due to retire now, but who would be staying on for a few more weeks, until Christmas, in order to hand over to his successor. As Laurel's eyes alighted on him he picked up a wooden gavel and banged it on the table for silence, smiling a welcome at the assembly as he did so.

'The old man's getting down to business right away,' the doctor next to her commented.

'We have a lot to get through in this meeting, so I don't propose to dilly-dally,' Dr Crayford announced bluntly, picking up the agenda in front of him.

'He never does dilly-dally,' Laurel's new companion muttered with a conspiratorial grin. She smiled back.

'There isn't much to say about the minutes of the last meeting, which I hope you will have read,' Dr Crayford said. 'I'll just go over the main points very briefly while we wait for our new chief of surgery to arrive—he called to say that he and his secretary would be a few minutes late. Some of you have already met Dr Jarrad Lucas, who has just spent a few months working in the Arctic. The rest of you will be introduced as soon as he gets here. . .'

Laurel spluttered into her coffee as some of the hot liquid went down the wrong way, and she felt a flush spreading over her face. The remainder of Dr Crayford's speech was lost to her, his lips mouthing words that she did not hear while she sat as though paralysed with shock. Why had Jarrad not told her?

Perhaps that was the reason for his long silence. Apart from a brief postcard from Mexico there had been nothing; not even after her three weeks' absence from the country, after she had decided impulsively to go to England to stay with her parents who now lived there.

Once back in Gresham, it had really come home to

her how little she knew about Jarrad's private life; she didn't even know his permanent address, and he had not been in the Gresham telephone directory. Although she could possibly have contacted him through the NMDC, she had been too proud to do so.

His continued silence, now that it was October, had left her feeling bitter—even though she had told herself time and time again that she had no claim on him.

Although she had so desperately wanted to see him...still did...she had not wanted it to be like this—that he should be her boss in this new place. He had known for some time that she had a job at this hospital. What a brilliant *fait accompli* on his part! What a clever act of revenge for perceived past wrongs...if that was what he wanted.

Pressing questions competed with each other for attention in her agitated mind; violent mixed emotions swung her from one extreme to the other as she strove unsuccessfully to focus her attention on the chairman of the meeting.

Through a window Laurel could see the car park where she had parked that morning. As she looked, as though she had willed the object of her thoughts to materialise at long last, a car drew up there and Jarrad got out of it, followed by a blonde woman.

As they walked towards the building that housed the meeting room where she sat Laurel could see that the woman was Ginny—a somewhat altered Ginny, more subdued in a very sophisticated way. She wore a russet-coloured suit of fine suede, the skirt coming down to just above her shapely knees, and her hips undulated suggestively as she walked on her high-heeled shoes.

Laurel turned her attention back to the room, aware that she had been holding her breath, that her heart rate had accelerated and that she felt slightly sick.

Feeling wretched with a sharp longing and jealousy, she waited for them to enter. At the same time she became determined not to show it; she would be damned if she'd let him see that she cared. Why on earth would Ginny be with him anyway?

The explanation was to come soon enough. After they had entered the room there was a general hubbub of greetings and introductions, so that no one noticed that she, Laurel, remained rigidly in her seat, her face expressionless. Ginny was introduced as Jarrad's secretary.

In spite of her resolve, Laurel's churning emotions were soon dominated by a sharp concern for Jarrad as her eyes remained fixed on him where he stood at the opposite end of the room. He did not look well; his normally lean face was frankly thin, his cheekbones more sharply accentuated by deep hollows beneath them. His eyes looked tired and strangely haunted, and although he had a faint tan to his skin, perhaps a legacy of Mexico, there was an underlying pallor.

Two seats had been kept for Jarrad and Ginny next to Dr Crayford, and as Jarrad sat down and the meeting progressed from where it had left off Jarrad looked at Laurel across the expanse of the vast table and gave a faint acknowledging smile. She did not smile back; too alarmed by his appearance, she could only stare.

With an unsteady hand she picked up her cup of coffee and began to sip it as the sounds of the speakers' voices drifted over her head unheeded. Briefly she surfaced, nudged into awareness when her name was mentioned and she was required to stand up while she was introduced to the assembly as a new staff member.

Whenever her eyes strayed back to Jarrad he was looking at her, his features in repose, telling her nothing. He had an arm flung casually along the back of the chair on which Ginny sat, where she looked every inch the efficient secretary, with pen poised above a pad of paper, her golden hair held back from her pert face with a floppy black silk bow.

Surely secretaries did everything by dictation now, Laurel found herself thinking rather sourly. Hard on that thought came the idea that Ginny was perhaps just going through the motions of being Jarrad's secretary. Perhaps they were actually married, had got married during the weeks when she had heard nothing from him. . .or perhaps they were lovers.

The anguish that she felt then was so powerful that she had an impulse to get up and run from the room. If she had not been far away from the door, which was just behind Jarrad, she would have done so. As it was, a conviction was coming to her that she could not work again with Jarrad. Feeling about him as she did, seeing that he was involved with Ginny, she would not be able to function properly in her job.

When the meeting paused for a snack and coffee-break, the doctors streamed out into an adjoining corridor where coffee-urns had been set up. Laurel moved out with them, and several of her new colleagues quickly came to talk to her, the men openly admiring and subtly curious. That morning she had taken trouble with her appearance, and knew that she looked both attractive and professional at the same time in a black and white houndstooth check suit and cream silk blouse.

In an interlude when she found herself briefly alone Jarrad was suddenly there beside her. 'Hello, Laurel.' He smiled down at her, his lean face creasing into the familiar lines that she loved, that she wanted to touch. . .to kiss. 'It's good to see you. How are you?' Quickly he bent down to kiss her on the cheek. 'A pity we have to meet in a crowd.'

'I'm fine,' she said, surprised at the crisp tone of

her own voice, trembling inwardly at the reality of his longed-for touch, and cynical about the fact that he could go through the motions so easily. Close up, she could see the deep lines of chronic tiredness on his face, and her incipient bitterness at having been apparently outmanoeuvred by him gave way again to concern for his health, and a poignant loss of hope for things that might have been between them. Now he had Ginny.

'What's more to the point, how are you?' she said, forcing herself to speak civilised words. 'You. . .don't look well, Jarrad. I expected to hear from you long ago, letting me know how you were.' She could not keep the slightly accusing note out of her voice, even though she was crying inside.

'After all, I was your original surgeon. And how come you're the chief of surgery here, all of a sudden? You didn't say a word of it in Chalmers Bay. . .that was very underhand of you, to say the least!'

'This was one of several jobs I'd applied for. I didn't know before I left Chalmers Bay that I'd got it. I haven't been particularly well since I was discharged from hospital. . . It's a long story, which I can't tell you here. Ginny's been looking after me. . .it was her choice,' he said, standing close, keeping his voice low.

'I don't think it will be possible for us to work together again, Jarrad,' Laurel announced in a subdued, trembling voice. 'It wouldn't work.' Those last words were the ones she had spoken to Joshua Kapinsky, for vastly different reasons.

'Why wouldn't it?' Jarrad looked at her astutely, his eyes searching her face as though he would read her soul once again.

'There seems to be a certain rivalry between us. . . still,' Laurel said bitterly. 'It's funny. . .we seem to have come full circle. I met Mr Foley in the lobby this morning, our cardiac arrest patient—the last one we saw together in Gresham...'

'I remember him,' he said, managing to let her know by his tone that he also remembered acutely every word that had passed between them after that incident. 'And as far as I'm concerned there's no rivalry between us.'

'I would like to resign my position here. I'll give it to you in writing tomorrow,' Laurel said impulsively, making up her mind.

Oblivious to everyone else around them, to the swell of conversation, they faced each other. What she really wanted to say to him would never be said now, she thought despairingly.

'That's very rash of you. Don't be silly,' he said, as though he were talking to a wayward child. 'I will not accept a resignation from you. Anyway, I'm only the nominal chief until Wilf Crayford finally goes at Christmas. You would have to give it to him...if you were stupid enough to do so.'

'Nevertheless, I would like to give it,' she insisted, moistening her dry lips with her tongue. 'Preferably to you.'

'No, you wouldn't,' he said, seeming to her to be peculiarly sanguine in his attitude. His eyes on her mouth were disconcerting her beyond measure. 'Besides, I wouldn't let you go without kissing you goodbye...and this is hardly the time or the place.'

Someone came up to claim his attention. 'We'll talk later, Laurel,' he said, moving away from her, 'You're going to be at Bonnie Mae's wedding in Edmonton next weekend?'

'Yes...why?' she said defensively.

'Don't do anything irrevocable before then. I'll talk to you there, if not before,' he said to her over his shoulder as he walked away, 'OK?'

Laurel did not answer as she watched him go. How could she trust him, even though she wanted to so much? Max had let her down so many times. After all, Jarrad had probably known Ginny longer than he had known her, and what man in his right mind would give up the delectable Ginny?

'Dr Haa-aarte.' Ginny was suddenly there beside her. 'Jarrad asked me to have a few words with you to...like...you know...set the record straight.' She drawled charmingly, in her familiar manner, on the verge of a giggle. 'It's really naa-aace to see you.'

'What record?' Laurel said abruptly, sick at heart.

'I'm not really Jarrad's secretary,' Ginny said airily. 'I'm just sort of standing in until he gets one. I guess you might have figured that out already.'

'I sure did,' Laurel drawled back, finding herself smiling wryly. Although Ginny was irritating in her apparent superficiality, there was something very likeable about her. Perhaps it was her childlike narcissism that brought out the latent parent in one, Laurel considered.

'Jarrad's been pretty sick,' Ginny went on. 'Got sick in Dallas on the way back from Mexico. I happened to be one of the flight attendants on the Cancún run, taking the flight to Dallas where we had a stopover. Pretty lucky I was there. He had a collapsed lung, right there on the aircraft, as we were coming in to land. They had to radio for an ambulance. It's a good thing that I'm a trained nurse. Did you know that I was a nurse, Dr Harte?'

'No, I didn't,' Laurel said abstractedly, shocked by the news and not ready to give kudos where they were evidently due.

'Sure am! I'm a Registered Nursing Assistant. When I wanted to get a job with an airline I was taken on straight away because of it...and because of the way

I look too, I guess,' Ginny said with a self-satisfied smile. Laurel wondered whether it would be possible for anyone ever to insult Ginny.

'I. . .I had no idea that Jarrad had had a collapsed lung,' she said, horrified, deciding to be perfectly honest with Ginny. There was no point in being otherwise. 'In fact, I haven't heard from him for a long time—which I'm rather annoyed about. He could have done me the courtesy of staying in touch. I was extremely worried about him.'

'Well, he was in no condition to do anything but lie flat on his back for a long time. He was in a real bad way in Dallas. . .a ree-aal bad way. He could have died there and then, right on that aircraft! It had something to do with that bullet wound he got in the shoulder. There was an infection as well.' Ginny widened her large, beautiful eyes and batted her eyelashes impressively to make her point.

'Oh, my God. . .I wish I'd known.'

'He wasn't making any phone calls or writing any letters, that's for sure!' Ginny went on dramatically at the same time as she fidgeted with the bow in her hair.

'I see. . .' Laurel said, thinking back soberly to her weeks of ignorance when Jarrad had obviously been seriously ill. 'And where do you come in to all this, Ginny? Are you and Jarrad getting married?'

Ginny gave a trilling laugh. 'Goodness, what a question! I sure would like to marry him, but he hasn't asked me.' She looked coyly sideways at Laurel. 'No. . .I don't think that's on the cards for me and Jarrad. We're just very good friends. . .verr-eee good friends.

'He operated on my mother two years ago. . .saved her life—for which I'll be eternally grateful. So will she, of course.' Ginny laughed again, delighted at her own wit. 'He was also engaged to my sister, Nicole. . .

she's an MD as well! That's how I met him. She must have been nuts to throw him over. I'd do anything for him...en-neee-thing!'

'I believe you,' Laurel said. 'I'm glad you were there when he needed someone. Why—er—why did your sister end the engagement?'

'She met a much older guy...really, really rich. That was what she wanted. She didn't love him—' Ginny laughed '—but she loved his money. They live in California now, and Nicole doesn't have to do a stroke of work unless she really wants to! Sometimes she works in a cosmetic surgery clinic, operating on famous people and film stars. Funny how things turn out, isn't it? Nicole was so-oo ambitious in med school...so-oo possessive of Jarrad too.'

The meeting resumed moments later, and continued until four o'clock in the afternoon. Laurel felt dazed with all the food for thought that Ginny had given her. There was no opportunity for her to talk to Jarrad during that time, so she waited afterwards in her parked car for him to come out to his own car before the drive back to Gresham. She had been wise, she contemplated now, not to have sold her apartment in Gresham before she had found out what the job in Riverton would be like, even though it meant commuting.

At last Jarrad emerged through a door, accompanied by a small group of his future colleagues. They stood around for some time, chatting, while Laurel seethed with impatience. She could see that Ginny had given up waiting for him and gone to sit in his car. When eventually he was free and walking with his swift, loping stride across the car park, attractive in a dark grey business suit, Laurel got out of her car and ran to intercept him.

'Why didn't you contact me...tell me that you had

a collapsed lung and an infection?' she said accusingly, not giving him a chance to utter a word first. 'Didn't you think I had a right to know?'

He didn't seem surprised by her question or her accusatory tone. 'I was in no condition to try to track you down,' he said. 'When I did eventually get through to someone in Gresham who knew you, they told me you'd gone to England and didn't know when you'd be back.'

Yes, that sounded very reasonable, Laurel conceded now, fully aware for the first time that she must have been as elusive to him as he had been to her after they had both left Edmonton.

'Why Ginny?' she asked. They were not talking about his illness now, or her job. They were suddenly in unknown territory, treading warily.

'She was there,' he said, 'when I was in need.'

'And I wasn't?'

'Precisely,' he said crisply.

'And what does she think about all this?'

'She feels she owes me one. I operated on her mother once. I never expected anything—it's just her way. There's nothing to it. I thought you might be married to old Josh by now.' He eyed her speculatively, a tenseness about him.

'I'm not.'

He ran a hand tiredly through his hair. 'Look, Laurel, we can't talk here. We've both got a lot to do. I'll see you at Bonnie Mae's wedding; we'll talk then. In the meantime, I'm not going to accept a resignation from you, and I'll ask Wilf Crayford not to do so either.'

He reached out and touched her cheek, then slid his hand quickly to the back of her neck, holding her head steady while he kissed her. Taken by surprise, Laurel merely closed her eyes against the autumn sun that was shining in her face as he tilted her head back. The full strength of her love held her passive.

How she had longed for his kiss in those weeks of separation, and now she could not disguise her helpless response, even in her desire to remain cool with him. They were in full view of the waiting Ginny. And, Laurel realised as Jarrad prolonged the contact, this could hardly be viewed as a kiss of friendship. A tentative feeling of hope for them insinuated itself into her consciousness.

Slowly they broke contact, oblivious to the watching Ginny, or anyone else who might have been walking across the car park. 'I've missed you. See you in Edmonton at the weekend,' he said huskily, moving back from her, managing to imbue the words, it seemed to her, with a certain promise that set her blood tingling throughout her body. 'Right?'

'Um. . .yes,' she murmured in reply. There was nothing else for her to say. She knew that he wanted her physically, knew that he was aware that she wanted him. It would have been hypocritical of her to pretend otherwise.

'Take care,' he said. He went then, away from her, and she watched him go, watched the car move out of the car park, out of the hospital grounds, and turn towards the main road to Gresham. The fact that Ginny was with him was of no importance.

For minutes she sat in her car, thinking. He had told her in Chalmers Bay that he was not ready to commit himself to a woman for at least another five years; his career came first. What would they talk about this weekend? And what would she do then?

CHAPTER ELEVEN

THEY were all there in the church—former staff who had worked with Bonnie Mae in the north, members of the RCMP, some of her friends from the village, Joe Fletcher, Dan McCormick, Skip.

Laurel looked around the large church that was packed with people, knowing for sure that Bonnie Mae was going to be right; this would be the best party she had ever been to. Clearly it was to be a traditional wedding—nothing trendy or newfangled for Bonnie Mae.

There were scented flowers everywhere, and the majestic sound of the organ overrode the buzz of muted conversation as the congregation waited for the bride to appear. Chuck, the bridegroom, huge and bearded, looking magnificent, if slightly self-conscious in a morning coat, waited at the altar with his best man.

As Laurel's eyes roved over the rows of people ahead of her in the congregation she recognised Josi Landers with her husband, then Rick Sommers. So far she had not seen Jarrad. When Bonnie Mae had telephoned her from Edmonton to talk about wedding arrangements she had said that Jarrad would be sitting next to her in the church. Bonnie had taken it for granted that she would want to be with him.

Now Laurel felt like a bride herself, sick with nerves and excitement, wondering why he had not yet come. Many times she had looked behind her, expecting to see him enter through the wide doorway of the church.

Bonnie Mae had also insisted on booking accommodation for her, telling her that some good friends of her family owned a hotel and country club—the Ranch Valley Country Club—and would 'just love' her to stay there—would give her special rates. Laurel had duly signed in that morning at the hotel, which was in a beautiful setting out of the city, and then she had had barely enough time to shower, dress for the wedding and get back to the church.

A peal of the organ, a prelude to the 'Bridal March', brought the congregation to its feet. Laurel turned sideways, with everyone else, to get a view of the aisle and Bonnie Mae on her father's arm.

There was a collective gasp of admiration as Bonnie Mae appeared—huge, regal, resplendent—in a glorious creation of cream-coloured satin that fell to the ground around her in many folds and to which a long train was attached, held by three page-boys and three small, beautifully dressed bridesmaids. There were four other bridesmaids, more mature, who fussed around Bonnie Mae, adjusting her veil, before she began her triumphant slow progression up the aisle.

Laurel felt a constriction of emotion in her throat and tears gathering, proud to know this remarkable yet modest woman. Modest about her accomplishments, that was. Trust Bonnie Mae to do this in style! Larger than life herself, it was only natural that she would make this the best party of her life.

As Laurel lifted her handkerchief surreptitiously to her eyes to dab at the tears she felt a hand touch hers, and as she turned the hand closed around hers in a firm grip from which she knew she would not be able to extricate herself.

'You're late,' she whispered, to hide her mingled joy and confusion, returning the pressure of his warm hand.

'Mmm. . .' Jarrad said, looking remarkably smug and very handsome as Laurel's eyes went over him admiringly. So used to seeing him in regulation work clothes that tended to be shapeless, she could not help staring at him openly now that he looked even more devastatingly attractive in a formal suit that fitted his lithe body like the proverbial glove.

Equally, his eyes were going over her attractive figure, once again as though he would like to devour her. The pale peachy-pink pleated and fitted chiffon dress that she wore clung to her in all the right places, suitably formalised under a long matching jacket and complemented by a wide-brimmed hat in the same colour.

'Do you like what you see?' Jarrad murmured in her ear as she was openly staring, pulling her up against him by the force of his hand in hers, showing his perfect white teeth as he smiled teasingly at her, knowing that she was at his mercy here in this crowded place.

Perhaps he could read in her face that she didn't want to get away, she thought heatedly. She felt as though she were melting with love for him. Utter relief at his arrival made her smile. 'Very much,' she admitted. Something very definite had happened between them, something that seemed like a miracle to Laurel just then in the emotionally charged atmosphere of the church with the swelling crescendo of music.

'You look very attractive, Laurel,' he said. 'Utterly delectable,' he added.

Laurel realised with agitated surprise that he was flirting with her—an activity that she had not imagined would sit easily with him. Yet he was doing it with an ease and panache that would have made anyone call it an art, even the most jaded. . .and it was nothing like the suggestive flirtatiousness that had been Joshua's signature behaviour. It was also doing things to her that she would never have imagined possible with Joshua Kapinsky.

They were two rows from the back of the church, next to a pillar, and thus partially hidden from people on one side of them. 'Where's Ginny?' Laurel said, articulating the words carefully, in competition with the organ.

'I've no idea,' he said, his head bent down under the brim of her hat so that his tingling breath sent a shiver of acute physical awareness through her. 'She wasn't invited.'

Then, as all attention was diverted to Bonnie Mae, he kissed her, willing her both physically and emotionally to an uncharacteristic quiescence. She dared not protest or struggle...and she did not want to.

When they were sitting side by side later for the service, Jarrad sat very close to her, his thigh against hers, still gripping her hand which he held close to his knee. At first Laurel held herself rigidly, not looking at him, feeling her face flush with heat; then very gradually, as the service progressed, she relaxed against him, her shoulder touching his. As she did so Jarrad loosened his grip on her hand and slid his arm around her waist, where she could feel the warmth of it under her jacket as he rested his hand lightly on her hip.

Once again the tang of his cologne filled her nostrils, reminding her of the time she had sobbed in his empty bed. Maybe one day she would tell him about that. As the service went on she leaned against him, her head against his shoulder, aware of little else but him and the fairy tale atmosphere of the decorated church.

It was past two o'clock in the morning when the car that Laurel had hired, with Jarrad at the wheel, turned into the long driveway that curved up to the sprawling two-storey building of the Ranch Valley Country Club.

The building was hidden from the road by mature

trees and lush vegetation, and a full moon cast a silvery glow over everything, seeming to accentuate the silence as the car came to a stop under the vast portico by the front door. There was no one else about, as far as Laurel could see.

'Are there other people here from the wedding, do you think?' Laurel asked Jarrad. 'It's awfully quiet. I had more or less expected a cavalcade of cars out in this direction from the reception.'

'I've no idea,' he said casually.

'When you said that Bonnie Mae had booked you in here as well as me, I thought this was to be the official hotel for the wedding,' she said. 'Oh...my head's really muzzy—' she put her hand up to her forehead '—too much champagne.' Laurel was chatting to disguise the tension and, she had to admit, the excitement that was mounting in her.

'Maybe only the medical profession could afford a place like this,' he murmured, teasing her. 'Think you can make it up to your room while I find a place to park this car?'

He leaned across her to open the door, bringing his face very close to hers so that she held her breath in anticipation. All evening they had danced together, and now she felt that her nerves were at screaming pitch; she was longing for Jarrad to crush her in his arms, to kiss her with that intense abandon she remembered.

'Mmm...I'm not that far gone—even though that was some party!' she said, wanting to ask him to come to her room but not knowing quite how to put it, still frightened of rejection. 'Will you...um...will you return the car keys to me...some time?'

'Sure,' he said.

On legs that felt as though they were made of feathers, she pushed through the impressive double doors into the spacious lobby and across to a reception desk where a young man, the night booking clerk, was talking on the telephone. 'Hello, ma'am.' He smiled at her, putting the telephone down to give her his full attention. 'Are we expecting you?'

'Oh, yes,' she said, 'I checked in this morning. Harte...that's my name. Room twenty-nine...you have the key.' Laurel supported herself against the edge of the polished reception desk, feeling her dizziness increase and her eyes go slightly out of focus as she peered at the board which held the room keys.

Not used to a lot of alcohol, she knew that she should not have drunk more than two glasses. The trouble with champagne was that you were liable to drink it like lemonade...'Is there some problem?' she asked of the clerk, who was looking at the guest register.

'Ah, now I have it,' the clerk said, frowning down at the register. 'Dr and Mrs Harte...booked into the honeymoon suite. That's you, right? You got married today, right? Well, congratulations, Mrs Harte, I wish you all the best. You're sure gonna love the honeymoon suite. It looks right over the valley...great view! Especially at sun-up! Not too much longer to wait now.' He chuckled, obviously thinking that they would be awake anyway until dawn.

'No...no...not my honeymoon,' Laurel said. 'It was Bonnie Mae...Mrs Melvin. There's some mistake...'

'Bonnie Mae, that's it! It was a Bonnie Mae somebody who booked it,' the clerk said triumphantly.

'There you are, then,' Laurel said, 'she booked it for herself. I'm in room twenty-nine. All my luggage is there.'

'There's no mistake, ma'am.' the clerk was looking determined, if as perplexed as Laurel felt. 'The booking was made for a Dr and Mrs Harte. It says so right here in the book. It also says that your luggage was transferred from room twenty-nine to the honeymoon suite this afternoon.'

'But. . .but I'm not, we're not. . .marr—'

'What's the hold-up, honey?' Jarrad was beside her suddenly, kissing her cheek, his arm possessively round her shoulders. 'Sorry to be so long; I had to drive around to the back to find a parking spot.'

'Jarrad, we've been booked into the the honeymoon suite by mistake—' she began, turning her head to look at him.

Jarrad kissed her on the mouth. 'It's all right, honey. That is the usual thing after a wedding.' He kissed her again, then turned to the bemused clerk. 'My wife's confused. Too much champagne! Besides, this is my little surprise for her. If you'll give me the key, I think we can find our own way there.'

'Right, sir. Take that elevator there to the second floor, then it's down the corridor to your right.' The clerk handed Jarrad the keys and Laurel found herself being walked across the carpet of the lobby towards two elevators, supported by Jarrad's arm firmly around her waist.

'What do you mean, your "little surprise". . .and "my wife"—?' she began. The words were cut off as Jarrad kissed her again, holding her against him easily with one arm. When the elevator came, he bundled her into it. As the doors closed he took her into his arms, holding the 'closed' button down with one finger behind her back. He was laughing openly now.

'I decided that with you, my dear Laurel, a bit of strong-arm stuff and subterfuge were the only things that would work. Saves a hell of a lot of talking,' he said.

'I think I'm beginning to see. . .' she said cautiously.

'Oh, what the hell...' Abandoning caution, she kissed him back, putting her arms round his neck, enjoying the heat of his body against hers, vaguely aware of the barely perceptible motion of the elevator as it moved upwards and then came to a gentle stop.

'Do you mind?' Jarrad queried softly as they got out of the elevator, hand in hand.

'No...' she said, even as a wave of shyness vied oddly with her elation, the delicious feeling of warm anticipation. 'I...don't think so.' Everything was happening too quickly for her; she felt herself being bowled along by an inevitable fate that she had only dreamed of.

Inside the magnificent honeymoon suite, with its dim lights and huge bed with rounded corners, wide enough for several people, Laurel tremblingly faced him, determined to say what she had to say before their mutual passion dimmed all reason.

'Jarrad...why didn't you contact me before just showing up at Riverton General? I was so worried, and I felt pretty stupid not knowing ahead of time that you were the new chief there.' It was hard now to resurrect the dismay she had felt then, now when she felt light-headed with love as well as champagne.

'For a lot of the time I was too sick. And later I wanted to give you plenty of time to sort yourself out with Joshua Kapinsky back in Gresham, without any influence from me.' They stood at the foot of the bed, facing each other, both hands linked, both still in their wedding finery. His deep, reasonable voice made it all ring true.

'I felt so lost without you...' she murmured, remembering.

Jarrad lifted one of her hands and kissed it. 'It wasn't easy for me, thinking you just might go ahead and marry the guy. I forced myself to do it...to give you a chance to sort it out for yourself. I went through absolute hell on that account. Are you over him, my love?'

'Yes. It was all a sort of hero-worship, really. It wouldn't have stood the test of time,' she explained, as much for herself as for him, as her love-filled eyes searched his face and found there the mirror of her own love. 'I never really wanted him. All the initiative came from him. . .he was a bit of a bully, really.'

'Do you want *me*, Laurel? I don't want all the initiative to come from me.' With his intensity he held her spellbound, reading her soul.

'Yes. . .' she said softly, her face breaking into a radiant, irrepressible smile, even though she wasn't sure exactly what she was consenting to. 'Oh, Jarrad, I was so worried, so lonely without you.'

'When I called Bonnie Mae one time, when you were in England,' he said, 'she let drop how you felt about me. So I knew I could bide my time until you sorted yourself out with Josh.'

'I wish you hadn't waited.' She went into his arms, resting her head against his chest, a swell of happiness overriding her remembered pain. 'Because I went through hell too.'

'Look at me, Laurel,' Jarrad commanded, holding her at arm's length. 'Bonnie Mae tells me that you're in love with me. Is that right?'

'Yes. . .'

'I've loved you for a hell of a long time,' he said, and to her amazement she heard his voice tremble. 'I was just too bloody-minded to admit it. . .and for a long time I thought you hardly knew I existed. Then there was Max. . .and Josh.'

'That's all in the past,' she said, suddenly sober. 'For the first time in years I can really look to the future.'

'With me?'

'Before I answer that...where does Ginny come into this?' Laurel said, equally tremulous. 'I have to know.'

'Ginny doesn't come into it. She's a family friend. I've never so much as kissed Ginny. I've never wanted to. Ginny is attractive, but looks are not enough... at least, not for me. To me, the lasting attraction is a woman's intelligence, her character. Your sort of intelligence, Laurel...and your personality, of course!'

'Oh, go on! I never knew you could be so smarmy!' Laurel gave him a playful push.

'Answer my question,' he insisted, his face intent with a fierce need.

'Jarrad, I love you.' She articulated each word carefully, gazing up at him adoringly. 'And, yes...yes to everything.'

By mutual unspoken consent they came together then in a long, sensual embrace, hungrily giving and taking from each other after what had seemed like a long drought, when love had been an elusive thing.

'As my original doctor,' Jarrad said, holding her away from him, 'I thought you might want to look at my scars—just as a sort of check-up. Hmm... Dr Harte?'

'Jarrad, you are an idiot sometimes.' She laughed. 'I guess that's why I love you so much. *Of course* I want to look at your scars! I thought you'd never ask!'

Later, as they lay side by side on the vast bed, with just a thin sheet between them and the warm air of the luxurious room, Laurel's fingers languidly traced the scars on Jarrad's shoulder as he held her possessively close to him.

'What happened to your five-year plan?' she murmured between kisses. 'Your earth-mother?'

'You can't plan for love,' he said huskily, tracing the outline of her lips with his thumb, sending shivers of anticipation through her. 'It takes you unawares. As for the earth-mother—she was your invention. . .'

'I'm so glad. . .'

'You know, going to Chalmers Bay was what we both needed. We needed that clarity of vision. What shall I call the experience? A prescription for love?' Jarrad murmured, pulling her close to him, enveloping her in his warmth.

'Yes. . .' Laurel agreed, smoothing her lips over the scar on his shoulder where the bullet had entered, knowing that a mysterious, uncontrollable fate had finally bound them together with a strong and lasting bond. 'And one that never has to be renewed.'

MILLS & BOON

For those long, hot, lazy days this summer
Mills & Boon are delighted to bring you...

Stolen Moments

A collection of four short sizzling stories in one romantic volume.

We know you'll love these warm and sensual stories from some of our best loved authors.

Love Me Not	Barbara Stewart
Maggie And Her Colonel	Merline Lovelace
Prairie Summer	Alina Roberts
Anniversary Waltz	Anne Marie Duquette

'Stolen Moments' is the perfect summer read for those stolen summer moments!

Available: June '96   Price: £4.99

Available from WH Smith, John Menzies, Volume One, Forbuoys, Martins, Woolworths, Tesco, Asda, Safeway and other paperback stockists.

GET 4 BOOKS AND A MYSTERY GIFT

FREE

Return this coupon and we'll send you 4 Medical Romances and a mystery gift absolutely FREE! We'll even pay the postage and packing for you.

We're making you this offer to introduce you to the benefits of Reader Service: FREE home delivery of brand-new Medical Romances, at least a month before they are available in the shops, FREE gifts and a monthly Newsletter packed with information.

Accepting these FREE books and gift places you under no obligation to buy, you may cancel at any time, even after receiving just your free shipment. Simply complete the coupon below and send it to:

MILLS & BOON READER SERVICE, FREEPOST, CROYDON, SURREY, CR9 3WZ.

No stamp needed

Yes, please send me 4 free Medical Romances and a mystery gift. I understand that unless you hear from me, I will receive 4 superb new titles every month for just £2.10* each postage and packing free. I am under no obligation to purchase any books and I may cancel or suspend my subscription at any time, but the free books and gifts will be mine to keep in any case. (I am over 18 years of age)

1EP6D

Ms/Mrs/Miss/Mr _____

Address _____

_____

_____ Postcode _____

Offer closes 30th November 1996. We reserve the right to refuse an application. *Prices and terms subject to change without notice. Offer only valid in UK and Ireland and is not available to current subscribers to this series. **Readers in Ireland please write to:** P.O. Box 4546, Dublin 24. Overseas readers please write for details.

mps MAILING PREFERENCE SERVICE

You may be mailed with offers from other reputable companies as a result of this application. Please tick box if you would prefer not to receive such offers.

MILLS & BOON

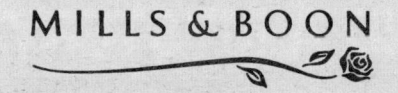

MEDICAL ROMANCE
LOVE ON CALL

The books for enjoyment this month are:

TENDER TOUCH	Caroline Anderson
LOVED AND LOST	Margaret Barker
THE SURGEON'S DECISION	Rebecca Lang
AN OLD-FASHIONED PRACTICE	Carol Wood

Treats in store!

Watch next month for the following absorbing stories:

A PRIVATE AFFAIR	Sheila Danton
DOCTORS IN DOUBT	Drusilla Douglas
FALSE PRETENCES	Laura MacDonald
LOUD AND CLEAR	Josie Metcalfe

Available from W.H. Smith, John Menzies, Volume One, Forbuoys, Martins, Woolworths, Tesco, Asda, Safeway and other paperback stockists.

Readers in South Africa - write to:
IBS, Private Bag X3010, Randburg 2125.